safe

safe

SUSAN SHAW

DUTTON BOOKS

DUTTON BOOKS
A member of Penguin Group (USA) Inc.

PUBLISHED BY THE PENGUIN GROUP

Penguin Group (USA) Inc., 375 Hudson Street, New York, New York 10014, U.S.A. / Penguin Group (Canada), 90 Eglinton Avenue East, Suite 700, Toronto, Ontario, Canada M4P 2Y3 (a division of Pearson Penguin Canada Inc.) / Penguin Books Ltd, 80 Strand, London WC2R 0RL, England / Penguin Ireland, 25 St Stephen's Green, Dublin 2, Ireland (a division of Penguin Books Ltd) / Penguin Group (Australia), 250 Camberwell Road, Camberwell, Victoria 3124, Australia (a division of Pearson Australia Group Pty Ltd) / Penguin Books India Pvt Ltd, 11 Community Centre, Panchsheel Park, New Delhi - 110 017, India / Penguin Group (NZ), 67 Apollo Drive, Rosedale, North Shore 0745, Auckland, New Zealand (a division of Pearson New Zealand Ltd) / Penguin Books (South Africa) (Pty) Ltd, 24 Sturdee Avenue, Rosebank, Johannesburg 2196, South Africa / Penguin Books Ltd, Registered Offices: 80 Strand, London WC2R 0RL, England

The poem "To a Daughter Who Worries Much" by Eileen Spinelli, which appears on pages 37–39, 46, 60–61, 137–139, 150, 151, 166–168, is used by permission of the author.

Library of Congress Cataloging-in-Publication Data
Shaw, Susan.
Safe / by Susan Shaw. — 1st ed.
p. cm.
Summary: When thirteen-year-old Tracy, whose mother died when she was three years old, is raped and beaten on the last day of school, all her feelings of security disappear and she does not know how to cope with the fear and dread that engulf her. ISBN 978-0-525-47829-4 (hardcover)
[1. Rape—Fiction. 2. Mothers—Fiction. 3. Security (Psychology)—Fiction.
4. Friendship—Fiction. 5. Schools—Fiction.] I. Title.
PZ7.S534343Saf 2007 [Fic]—dc22 2006036428

Published in the United States by Dutton Books, a member of Penguin Group (USA) Inc.,
345 Hudson Street, New York, New York 10014 www.penguin.com/youngreaders

Designed by Heather Wood / Printed in USA / First Edition 10 9 8 7 6 5 4 3 2 1

WITH LOVE TO

MARCIASUSANDAVIDJOHNANDNANCY

AND TO ALL THAT MEANS

ACKNOWLEDGMENTS

Many thanks to Eileen Spinelli for her friendship and for allowing me the use of her wonderful poem. Also thanks to Terry VanHook and to my husband for their invaluable critiques. Much appreciation to Lieutenant Albert Vagnozzi of the Upper Merion Township Police and to Dr. Margaret Blaustein for their professional input. And huge, huge bouquets to my editor, Julie Strauss-Gabel.

safe

"Baby freeze her fingers, baby freeze her fingers."

"I know, Tracy." The little girl's grandmother shifted the child's weight against her hip. "We'll get you warm soon." She looked at her son. "Rob? Robert?"

"Baby freeze her fingers," Tracy said again. She gripped an untasted oatmeal cookie. "Baby freeze her fingers."

"Are you ready, Rob?" the grandmother asked. "Tracy's cold."

This small family stood at the Pennsylvania graveside of Georgeanne Winston that March day. So pale was Robert Winston that his freckles stood out starkly against his skin, and the little girl had to keep looking at him to make sure he really was Pa.

Robert touched the casket one last time before moving away, before moving toward the funeral parlor's waiting limousine. His mother followed, carrying the little girl.

I was the little girl.

1.

IN THE YEARS FOLLOWING MAMA'S FUNERAL, HER PERFUME SOMEtimes wafted through my bedroom window, and she floated in on its moonbeam scent. It wasn't very often, and more times when I was little than later. She nestled me in her arms, keeping me safe, smoothing my black curls with her caress, whispering how beautiful I was getting.

The thing that cracked when she died was mended, and we were fine and whole again. And because we were fine and whole, I was safe. She would tell me the old stories, but I could never remember them later except for this ending from my favorite one:

The wind blew wild and the wind blew free, but the bear cub was safe in the mouth of the mama-mama bear.

That's the way I felt when Mama held me—*safe in the mouth of the mama-mama bear.* If I had trouble sleeping at night, I remembered the feel of the story—*safe in the mouth*—and I felt my mother in her pretty yellow dress, and the yellow rose pinned in her dark hair, and her arms around me. Then I could relax and know I was fine.

So even though I knew Mama died, I also knew in a way I never tried to explain to anybody that she didn't die, that she couldn't have, not completely, since she came to me with those moonbeam visits.

Another person might say that her visits were dreams, but I knew they weren't. Mama surrounded me with her love and light and perfume and kept me safe.

That was no dream.

Safe. Safe and warm in the mouth of the mama-mama bear. Safe.

———

Then on the last day of seventh grade, June fifteenth it was, I stepped across an invisible break on the way home from school. I didn't see it or know it was there, but when I crossed over it, I wasn't safe anymore. It was only late morning because all we'd done was have one last awards assembly, collect our report cards, and go home. We didn't even have lunch first.

As usual, I was walking home with Caroline, my best friend.

As usual, I said, "Seeya," when we reached her yard.

As usual, she answered back, "Seeya, Trace."

As usual. It was all as usual.

From the sidewalk, I watched Caroline take her everyday path across the grass to her front door. I continued on, aiming for home six houses farther down the Third Avenue hill and across the street. I didn't bother to turn a couple of seconds later when I heard Caroline's front door slam in that dry way that doors slam. *Why would I?*

That dry slam, it was part of what tacked my universe in place. It meant Caroline was inside her house, just where she was supposed to be. Like normal. I didn't need to look to know that she was all right, the way I didn't have to check to see that the sun was in the sky. Things were the way they were supposed to be.

But Caroline was no longer with me.

This is very important.

She was with me, and then she wasn't. Everything still felt like normal. Only it wasn't.

I stepped across the break like everything was all right, and the thing that had cracked when my mother died, the thing that was mended over and over with her love and warmth and caresses and stories, the thing most precious to me, shattered.

It shattered and I didn't know it. Wouldn't you think I would have heard it or felt it or seen it? Something that important? But I didn't. And because I didn't, I just kept on walking like everything was good and fine.

After it all happened, I went over and over that last minute, and I could never come up with anything that said, *Tracy! Watch out!* Even Caroline's slammed green door didn't say that—but it should have.

I kept on down the sidewalk. *Tomatoes,* I was thinking. *Tomatoes and cheese and that good bread Pa bought at the bread store. And milk. I'll put the sandwich on that blue plate with the raised white flowers and then—*

CCRRR!

I jumped a foot!

An orangey car with rust all over it—*where'd it come from?*—bubbled out of the blacktop, crunching the curb at my ankles before lurching to a stop.

Idiot! I thought. *Can't you drive?*

I kept my head turned so the driver couldn't see the disgust on my face. I stepped toward the grassy edge of the sidewalk. I was lucky he didn't hit me.

It scared the heck out of me, but why should I be scared? I was big now, not little. Thirteen years old and five-nine. I could have passed for a college kid, maybe, to some people, that's how mature I looked. I was *thirteen.*

When I glanced back, I was surprised to see someone I knew. Roddy Newman's brother. I knew him . . . or at least I knew who he was. I'd seen him once when he came to our school with the high school choir.

Roddy'd waved at his older brother that afternoon, shouting, "Burgess! Burgess!" but Burgess never looked away from the video equipment he was setting up.

Roddy'd glanced around at everyone sitting near him, including me. "That's my brother," he announced, but no one needed telling. Burgess looked so much like Roddy, I thought he was Roddy when I first saw him, except Roddy was right by me, making all that noise to get his brother's attention.

Like Roddy, Burgess was tall and on the chunky side with straight blond hair falling over his glasses and a face that made me think he'd just eaten a lot of salt. But Burgess was taller than Roddy by at least six inches; Burgess was well over six foot.

So the driver of the orangey car was Burgess, the kid who ran the video equipment while the high school choir sang. Roddy's older brother who'd pretended he didn't hear Roddy calling to him. Not exactly a stranger.

I thought Burgess was going to ask me where someone in the neighborhood lived or something like that. But he didn't say anything at all. He stepped out of the car and went straight to the door behind it, as though he had to pull something out of it, fast. Like an angry cat.

I kept walking. What did I care what Burgess was doing? It had nothing to do with me. That's what I thought. I didn't like how close he'd stopped his car, scraping those tires inches from me, but I didn't think that it meant anything.

Then—touch. Grab*YANK!*

No time to whirl around or demand, "What are you doing?!" or scream bloody murder or holler or anything. No time.

I sailed through space to crash into corners and sharp edges where the back seat of the car should have been. *Slam! Slam!* The car accelerated *fast,* bouncing me against unforgiving metal like a forgotten loaf of bread. *Bounce, bounce, bounce!* Ow! Oh! *Owwww!*

I—

I won't think about the rest.

———

When I was eleven, a gigantic wave pounded me on the rocks at Locust Point, pounding me over and over and over again.

Air! Air!

I swallowed water and panicked. *He-e-elp!* Finally, a breaking wave tossed me far up on the shoreline and washed away, leaving me in a shrinking sandy hole. Choking and hurting with a broken arm, I climbed over the rocks, and climbed and climbed before falling into the dry reeds in front of Grammum's bungalow. I stayed there for a long time, just glad the waters of the angry ocean couldn't find me again to finish me off.

———

What happened with Burgess Newman was worse than that. But I won't think about it.

After, there was a blank, and the next thing I remember

is walking down some street. I didn't even know most of my clothes were gone. I didn't feel that at all. I was bleeding and I didn't know that, either. Totally out of it, that's what I was, just walking, dazed in the bright afternoon sun, not knowing where I'd been the minute before, not knowing where I was going, not knowing where I was, hardly knowing who I was, just holding a movie in my head. A movie with a bunch of still frames of someone who looked like me being dragged right arm first out of the orangey car's trunk and tossed across a falling-apart pavement.

Me. It was me in those pictures.

Bang! The trunk slammed shut, and the noise of it hurt my head. *Screeeech!* The car took off, and I felt the reacting wind and the sting of cinders and broken glass.

Another car screeched. I blinked and there it was, bearing down on me. I felt the wind from that, too, and someone shouted, but I couldn't organize the shout into meaning.

Another blank.

———

"My God!" It was Pa, looking down at me. I looked down at me, too. I was wearing this funny kind of nightgown. It had blue diamonds with dots in every center. Faded blue diamonds with dots. Dots.

"I don't understand," I said to Pa. "What is—?" I looked around. "What is anything? What? Um?"

A hospital emergency room. That's what Pa said.

He held me and told me he loved me and that everything would be fine, and that they'd get the person who did this to me. Having him hold me like that was the only good thing out of it all, having him hold me and being right there with me. I just wished he could have held me harder and tighter and made the bad feelings, the dirty feelings, go away. But I don't think you can hold a person that tight, so tight that she's in your heart, way inside your skin, being cleaned and warmed by your blood.

2.

"YOU'LL WANT TO WAIT IN THE WAITING ROOM," THE POLICE DETEC-
tive said to Pa. Lily was her name.

"I will?" he asked.

"Trust us," said Maureen. She was a counselor from the
women's center. Someone there to look after my interests, she'd
said, like an aunt or a big sister—to help me be comfortable.
Was that possible? "Trust us," she repeated. "It will be easier. On
both of you."

Pa looked at me. "Want me to stay, punkin?"

Well, I did, but I told him to go. Lily and Maureen were
going to ask me to talk about things I didn't want to say in
front of him. Him or anybody. But I had to say them.

"Okay," said Pa., "but if you change your mind, I'll be right
nearby."

Maureen walked Pa to the door. "There's coffee out there,"
she told him. "Probably some doughnuts, too. If you need anything, just ask."

He nodded and left the room. That left me with two people
I didn't know. Left me there wearing clothes that didn't fit and
weren't even mine.

"They're clean," the nurse at the hospital had told me, "just
not very nice." So I could leave without Pa having to make a
round-trip to our house and back first.

Now I sat in a room in the police station that could almost
have been someone's living room, wanting to get it all over with

so I could go home and take a shower and have some hot chocolate and sit in *my* living room. My safe living room.

"So," said Lily. "Today was the last day of school, wasn't it?"

"Yeah," I said. "Just a half day. We didn't even have lunch."

"You were going to go home and have lunch?"

"Sure. But I didn't get there."

"What happened?"

And then it all was like—so awful.

Lily kept asking questions, and I kept answering, but I felt like I was in some kind of noisy furnace with black and red all around me. Noisier and blacker and redder. I could hardly feel the room I was in. Redder and blacker and hotter and full of ashes—

"Hold it," came a voice from outside the ashes. I blinked. It was Maureen talking. The ashes and the funny colors faded some. "Are you all right?" she asked. She was bent over me, her dark eyes searching mine.

I blinked at her a bunch of times. "I feel like someone keeps turning on and off the lights."

"Put your head down," she said.

I did, but inside my crooked arms, I said, "I want to finish. I want to say what I have to say and go home."

"We'll finish," said Lily, "but we can be kind."

After a minute, I lifted my head. "Could I just have some water?" I asked.

Maureen pointed to the table where a pitcher and filled glasses sat. They'd been there all along. Maureen lifted a glass to me, and I took it. I drank from it and drank from it. That water tasted so good!

"All right," I said. I put the empty glass down. "I can go on."

Maureen sat again, and we continued. Question, answer, question, answer. I was glad Lily was doing it that way. It just would have been so hard to tell the story straight through without the questions.

"All right," said Lily after a while. "We have all we need. We'll arrest the man."

"Man? Burgess is a kid."

"He's over eighteen," said Lily.

Maureen stood up. "I'll call your father in now and we'll discuss what the two of you can expect next."

Then we all sat together while Lily and Maureen talked with Pa. They talked with me, too, but I couldn't listen anymore. What I remember is the hum of quiet conversation that dodged around me but didn't form into words. Mostly, I concentrated on Pa's familiar smell that circled me while his arm held me tight. His familiar Pa-smell and the rumble of his voice when once in a while he asked a question.

So when Pa and I left, I didn't know what they'd all said. What was important was that we were outside the police station now and walking toward our car. And that Pa's arm was still around me, tight around me. That was most important.

"Are they going to arrest him?" I asked.

"That's exactly what they're going to do," said Pa. "Right now. I bet they have him before we get home."

I thought about that, about how Burgess might get arrested in his family room while he was watching television. Or eating a hamburger at a McDonald's. Or having a catch with Roddy in his backyard.

"It's not fair," I said to Pa.

"What's not fair?"

"How he's out there acting like nothing's wrong. Watching

14

television or playing baseball. Maybe packing for a vacation. Like nothing happened."

"Oh, something's wrong, that's for sure," said Pa. "If he doesn't think so, he's about to find out. But you're right. It's not fair. That's one thing it isn't."

In the car, I said, "Pa, do I have to do anything else? I mean with the police."

"You'll have to talk to people in the district attorney's office. Just like you did today, only with different people. That'll be all. For now. Because they need to hear what you say, too, to build the case."

"Okay."

We left the parking lot and drove into traffic. Telephone poles whipped by. Pole-pole-pole-pole. Pole-pole-pole-pole. There was something Pa said—*what was it?*

For now.

"What do you mean, for now?" I asked. Pole-pole-pole-pole.

And Pa explained about how there was one thing that would happen immediately without me. Then two things much later—weeks, months later—that probably I wouldn't have to be part of. I might, but probably not. Not either of them.

Either, neither, unbeliever. What? I blinked hard. Pa's last words echoed around me. *Not either of them.*

"Uh-huh." I watched the green light in front of us turn yellow as we stopped, then red. Then green, then yellow, then red. Then green. "Pa?"

"Just thinking hard." Pa eased the car forward and the telephone poles whipped by once again. Pole-pole-pole-pole. Pole-pole-pole-pole.

The arraignment, the preliminary hearing, and the court

appearance. They were the three things that had to happen. Pa kept explaining because I kept not hearing it.

Finally, I put it together. The arraignment would be the thing that day without me.

"Probably you won't have to go to the preliminary hearing, either," said Pa. "That's usually waived."

"Waved." I pictured the courthouse making itself into waves like the ocean and crashing onto the concrete sidewalk. I knew Pa didn't mean that, but the bricks crashed and foamed red against the hard concrete just the same.

"Waived," said Pa. "Bypassed. Not happening."

"Not happening." Like a parrot.

Pa glanced sharply at me. "Do I need to stop? You're not going to faint or anything, are you?"

I shrugged. "No. I'm just feeling spacey."

"Me, too."

And the last part, the court appearance. I wanted to know about it, so I kept asking Pa. He was so patient, and he kept telling me even though after the first five words, his voice kept melting into the car engine and turn-signal clicks. But I wanted to know it. I wanted to know if I could just leave it all behind me. I wanted to know.

Finally, I got it. Unless Burgess pleaded not guilty in front of the judge in the Court of Common Pleas, I wouldn't have to go to that, either.

"He has to plead guilty," I said.

"I bet he does." Pa pulled our car into the driveway and we went inside. Home! It never looked so good!

I don't know what happened all the rest of that afternoon, except for a long shower and some of Pa's special hot chocolate. Such rich, deep chocolate that you almost need a spoon to eat it. And the smell of it! That was half of what I wanted. The smell to fall into like the best kind of dream.

At dinnertime, the phone rang, and Pa answered it.

"I see," he said. "Thank you. Right. Good-bye." He turned to me. "They got Burgess Newman. He admitted everything, and they had the arraignment. He couldn't make bail, so now he's in prison. He's off the streets."

"Good," I said. "So that part's over."

"Yup," said Pa. "That part's over." He pushed his green beans into his mashed potatoes, then his mashed potatoes into his green beans. He looked at me over the mess and put the fork down. "Let's forget this and put on a Marx Brothers movie."

We left dinner right where it was on the table. We weren't eating it, anyway.

In the living room, we watched *A Night at the Opera*. Well, it played on the television set, but I didn't watch it really. Not really.

I never saw Lily or Maureen again, but Pa talked to them once in a while. I didn't want to. I was finished with the police. Then, after another week, I was also finished with the people from the district attorney's office. I told them all the same stuff that I'd said to Maureen and Lily.

I did all of that—talked to everybody I was supposed to, went over all the information about what happened on June fifteenth. *But so what?*

I was glad that Burgess Newman wasn't walking around outside anymore. That counted. A lot. If only I could *feel* that it was true. But I couldn't.

Burgess was around every corner every second. And my

bruises and cuts and stitched-up places—they didn't stop hurting. All that I could have stood if it was the worst part. But it wasn't the worst part.

The worst part was that what Burgess Newman did to me made it so Mama never came back.

The cracked piece that always mended when I was with her shattered and made the air cold. Shattered like the most delicate crystal and never came together again.

Mama's visits ended.

I'd lie under the covers at night and breathe in deeply, breathing in to catch the faintest honeysuckle-and-moonbeam scent, and nothing would be there. The air felt icy and hollow and tight. Too tight to let Mama in.

I couldn't even think of Mama and the yellow rose and the yellow dress or the way her stories felt. I couldn't get into the *zone* to remember it. I could say it and write it down—*Mama wore a yellow dress. She pinned a yellow rose in her dark hair*—I could do that. I could say that, but I couldn't *get* it.

How could I *get* it again? How could I fix the shattered piece?

3.

JUNE SIXTEENTH WASN'T A MONDAY OR A TUESDAY OR ANY DAY like that. It was an afterwards day with no name, and Pa and I both slept late. Then in our bathrobes, we sat cross-legged on the living-room floor playing war the rest of the morning.

War is the most boring card game in the world, but we played it anyway, Pa drinking coffee and me drinking hot chocolate.

We started the game with jack, two. Mine.

Nine, seven. Pa's.

Four, four. War.

Then one, two, three, queen, one, two, three, six. Pa's.

He took his pile while I swirled the hot chocolate under my nose and breathed it in. Breathed it in and time let go and everything felt funny, and suddenly the carpet didn't seem real, and I had to touch its roughness to make sure.

Pa was looking at me. "What?" I asked. Of course it was real. What was I thinking? But nothing felt real. I touched the carpet again.

"Aren't you going to play your card?" asked Pa.

I looked down. An ace of hearts. I threw down a four. Pa reached for the trick.

"Wait," I said.

Pa paused. "It was my ace, wasn't it?"

"Oh, yeah," I said, "you won the trick. It's not that. I just remembered something."

"What?"

Then—*blip!*—it went away. "Um, I forget." I threw down a card and stared at the bicycle rider in red ink. Silly-looking bicycle. When did bikes look like that? Pa's hand reached across and turned the card over. A seven. "Oh." I grinned foolishly. "I forgot."

"It helps just a bit to be able to see the other side."

Then I remembered what *blipped* away.

"My school year finished before yours," I said. "Philly has another week."

"Yeah. So?" Pa took my seven and his nine and and pushed them into his pile. "Trying to rub it in?"

"No. I mean. Did you forget to go in?"

"No, I didn't forget to go in," he said. "I took the day off."

"But—" I felt so confused. "You never take a day off." I stared at him. "Unless I'm sick. Am I—am I missing something?"

He laughed. Was his laugh a little louder than usual? "Don't look so shocked," he said. "A man can take a day off once in a while. But I should probably go in tomorrow if you're okay with that."

I stroked the carpet. It was real. I was real.

"You could have gone in today." Then I thought about that. "Well, maybe not."

"Not," he said. "Both of us needed to play war this morning."

He put out his next card. Jack. Mine was a seven, and he won again.

"Cheater," I said.

"Huh!"

Four, six. Mine. I swept the played cards into my pile and took a sip of the chocolate.

"How are you feeling today?" Pa asked.

"Truthfully?"

"Truthfully."

I stared into my mug for a minute before answering. Then I rested it on my knee, my hands still around it, absorbing the warmth against my palms. "I keep feeling like—I don't know, like I'm stuck in an elevator, and I can't get the elevator to go down. I just want it to go down, and I'm stuck up there between the third and fourth floors."

"The elevator'll come down," said Pa. "It'll take a while, but it will come down."

I squeezed my hands tighter on the mug, flattening out the curves and angles against the warm smoothness of the ceramic. "I keep trying to think what I could have done differently. So that guy didn't grab me."

"That's a useless exercise."

"But it was broad daylight. Don't these things usually happen in the dark? When nobody's around? Mr. Proctor could have been sitting in his front yard with his dog. Lots of times he's there." I paused and stared again into the chocolate. "Just not yesterday. I guess because it was morning."

I paused again, upper teeth over my lower lip.

"But he could have been," I finally went on. "He could have been there. The mailman could have been walking up the street. Or the Grayson twins could have been drawing with chalk on the sidewalk like they sometimes do. That guy—" I didn't like to say his name. "How could he have known?" I moved my mug onto the carpet and let go of it. I looked at Pa. "How could he have known?"

Pa sipped his coffee. "I don't think any of that mattered to him. He was just going to do what he was going to do." Then he told me about a Mob killing that happened in Philadelphia a long time ago. "A pair of hit men were driving in a car. They shot their victim and right away got arrested because a couple of cops were driving in traffic right behind them."

"The hit men never even looked in the rearview mirror?"

"Apparently not."

"Huh!" I thought about that. "I guess they were surprised."

Pa raised his eyebrows. "You might say that. It would be funny if the guy hadn't actually been killed."

"Yeah. They were stupid." I tossed out a card. "I wish there'd been policemen driving behind that orangey car yesterday."

"Me, too."

Then I saw the car and felt the air and— "I don't want to talk about it anymore." I said it fast.

We went back to playing war, but after a while, we took longer and longer between turns, and finally just sat there staring.

After a long silence, Pa got to his feet. "I quit," he said.

"Me, too."

"I'm going upstairs to get dressed," he told me. "I can stand a bathrobe only so long."

I nodded and listened to Pa's feet rising on the steps. I sat among the war piles, staring into space and swirling the hot chocolate in my mug.

Tap! to my head.

I looked fast in seventeen different directions.

Never mind. Only Pa's gentle touch. But my heart was racing. Only Pa, only Pa.

"I'm sorry," he said. "I thought you saw me when I came back down."

"No big deal," I said. I smiled at him. *See?* Absolutely present. Real. Like the carpet.

"Call Caroline," he said. "Call Caroline and get dressed."

"I don't want to," I said. "I don't want to talk to anybody." I drank the rest of the chocolate and stood up.

"You're not going to talk to anybody at all?"

"How can I talk to Caroline with my face all messed up the way it is?"

"A girl needs her friends at a time like this," Pa said. He handed me the cordless. "You'd want her to call you if it had happened to her, wouldn't you?"

So I called Caroline. "Can you come over? I want to talk to you about something."

"Give me ten minutes," she said, "and I'll be down."

So I quick went upstairs and changed into some jeans and a long-sleeve T-shirt. The legs and sleeves of my clothes felt snug against my sores, soothing, so I liked that. But I felt cold, so I pulled a sweatshirt over my head. *Still* cold, so I put on a fleece jacket. I couldn't get rid of the cold feeling, but since I was starting to sweat, too, I stopped with the layers.

How can I sweat when I'm cold?

After descending the steps again, I opened the front door and watched, holding on to the doorknob, as a form in turquoise—Caroline in her favorite windbreaker—loped down the street with her head tilted the way it always did when she ran. It felt so good to see her doing something so ordinary. As she neared, the softness of her features sharpened into her face, and it felt so good to see that, too. Caroline.

When she reached our walk, she slowed her pace, and I waited where I was. I didn't want to let go of the doorknob.

"What's up?" Caroline asked, all cheery. Then she caught sight of my face. Her eyes widened and her mouth dropped open. "Tracy! What in the world happened?"

23

Automatically, I put a hand over my face, trying to cover the worst of it while also avoiding the sorest place over my right eye. "Gruesome, isn't it?" I withdrew my hand and tried to smile. "I'm auditioning to play Mrs. Frankenstein."

"But, Tracy—"

"I'll tell you in a minute." I led her through the house to the kitchen door. "Come out to the pond with me." I wanted to talk to her without Pa hearing.

At the counter, Pa paused in his coffee pouring. "Hi, Caroline," he said.

"We'll be at the pond," I told him. I opened the back door and looked across to the pond that bordered our yard, and suddenly I knew there was nothing in the world that was going to get me to walk out there. Not if I couldn't see Pa. I turned to him. "Can you come out, too? Just to the patio? Please?"

"Sure, punkin." Pa followed us out as far as the picnic table with his coffee. "I'll be right here," he said. "Give me a shout if there's any problem."

"Problem?" Caroline repeated as we walked through the dry grass. She gave me a funny look. "What problem could *we* ever have?" she asked.

I looked back at Pa. Caroline looked back, too. Pa raised his mug to me encouragingly.

"Pa's all right," I said.

"He looks all right, but he's acting all weird, same as you. Were you both in a car accident or something?"

And that made me laugh, only what came out didn't really feel like laughter.

"You sound funny, Trace. What's going on? Why is your face all cut up?"

When we reached the pond, I looked back at Pa again. Not

so far. He could get to me in two seconds, running, if anything happened, so I was all right. Maybe four seconds. But nothing was going to happen. Burgess wasn't going to rise up out of the water. He was in jail. Still, I was glad Pa was there, right there. Because you don't ever really know where another person is if you're not looking directly at him.

"What is it, Tracy?" Caroline asked.

I scooped up a pebble and dropped it from hand to hand before letting it slip between my fingers.

Then I went ahead and said it.

"Something happened." I told Caroline as fast as I could. Told her the short, clean version. Enough. So I didn't have to think about it any longer than necessary.

"My God! *Roddy's* brother did that? *Roddy's* brother?"

I nodded.

Caroline paced a small circle, her fists clenched. "No. Oh, Tracy. Tracy. I shouldn't have gone inside when we got to my house yesterday. I should have walked you the rest of the way down the hill."

"Oh, come on. You never do that. Why would you start then? And afterward, I would have had to turn around and walk you back to your house so you wouldn't be alone. If we were afraid like that."

She looked at me. "Your face, Tracy. He really hurt your face."

I glanced down at my long pants and long sleeves. "And everything else. I'm pretty beat up all over."

Caroline stood staring at me, shaking her head, sinking down onto the bank. I sat beside her.

"What can I do?" she asked. "How can I help?"

"Just be here," I said. "Don't let me be alone."

"I won't."

25

"Promise?"

"Promise."

We sat quietly by the pond for some time, just staring at the water. Pa's mug made a scraping sound against the picnic table, so I didn't need to look to know he was there. Nothing was going to happen. What could happen? But Pa was there, and that was important.

Caroline had a reedy stalk that she bent over and over in her hands until it was hardly there. Then she discarded it and started on another. A ghost ran over my grave, and I shivered.

"Cold?" Caroline asked. "It's warm out today, and you're wearing stuff for winter. A jacket, even."

"I can't get warm," I answered. "The sleeves and pants press against my sores and make them feel better, but I'm still cold."

Caroline took off her windbreaker and put it around my shoulders.

"Now *you're* cold," I said.

"Not me." She went back to bending the stalk. "My mother's the cold one. She wouldn't let me leave the house without a jacket." Caroline threw the stalk aside. "I'll kill Burgess Newman," she said. Her voice was quiet. Intense, but quiet.

"The cops got him," I said. I pulled my knees up and hugged them tight to my chest. "He admitted it all, and he's in jail."

"Lucky for him," said Caroline. "Lucky for him he's not near me."

"Thanks, Caroline." I looked across at my friend. "He thought I was dead when he hauled me out of his trunk. I could tell. He meant to kill me, and I'm not sure why I'm alive."

Caroline picked up a good-size stone from the bank and showed it to me.

"This is Burgess Newman," she said. She stood up and threw it as far as she could. We watched it curve over the pond and splash way out there.

"No." I stood up and found another rock, a bigger one than Caroline had chosen. It had orangey stripes running through it. "*This* is Burgess Newman."

I started to throw it, but *"Ow!"* the pain in my shoulder and arm spiked, and I dropped the stone. "Ow!" I held my right shoulder with my left hand. Gently because the bruise there was like jelly. How could I have tried to throw that rock?

The rock rolled jaggedly down the bank before getting caught in a niche halfway to the water. It rocked there back and forth, back and forth. My eyes met Caroline's.

"Oh, well," I said. "You get the idea."

Caroline walked down after the rock and picked it up. "Is this still Burgess Newman, Tracy?"

I nodded. While I watched, Caroline heaved it after the first one. Not as far, but it was heavy.

Spa-loosh!!

The orangey rock made a hole in the water as big as my head, sending out a spray that reached way out, but not far enough to get us. Then the spray fell on the water, and Burgess Newman was history. That Burgess Newman.

"He's gone," Caroline said.

"Down to hell," I added. "Never to return."

We stared at the spot until the ripples smoothed out.

"Let's go to my house." Caroline's voice was bright. "My mom was making oatmeal cookies when I left. Let's go eat them all."

"Baby freeze her fingers."

"What?"

I blushed. "It just slipped out."

"Baby does what?"

"It's what I said at my mother's funeral." I bit my lower lip, still feeling kind of funny about it. "*Baby freeze her fingers, baby freeze her fingers.* I was holding an oatmeal cookie when I said it. That's what made me think of it." I tried to grin. "You pushed a button from the past when you mentioned oatmeal cookies."

"Well, this cookie tasting isn't at a funeral," Caroline said. "It's at my house, and we're going to eat cookies and shoot baskets and then we're going to eat more cookies."

But I couldn't. I knew that. I couldn't go to Caroline's—not all that way from the house. Not without Pa.

"I can't, Caroline," I said. "I have to stay here. Can you understand?"

"Sure. What I understand is this. I'm getting cookies and bringing them down. That's what I understand. And we'll eat cookies and shoot baskets in your driveway and eat more cookies. How about that?"

We giggled, and that clicked everything into place to feel fine and ordinary. *The heck with Burgess Newman* is what I thought. *The heck with this kind of crud.* And as Caroline rounded the side of our house and up the street for the cookies, I felt really pretty good. Good ol' Caroline, making me feel like an ordinary person again.

I sat at the picnic table with Pa and smiled at him.

"Caroline's bringing us cookies," I said. "Oatmeal."

Pa raised his mug. "Here's to Caroline," he said.

4.

I WOULD HAVE SLEPT IN THE NEXT MORNING, BUT FOR SOME REA-
son, I was up with the birds and waiting for Pa when he came
down for breakfast. I laughed at his wide eyes and raised brows
when he came into the kitchen.

"I was being so quiet upstairs, too," he said, "so I wouldn't
wake you."

"Fooled you," I said.

Pa cooked up some French toast and served it with maple
syrup and strips of bacon and orange juice. Just smelling it—
smelling it with my eyes closed while Pa sat across the table—
that was all I needed. And I ate three pieces of French toast.

"This is delicious," I said.

"Some days," Pa said, "call for that special touch. Now, listen, I can call out today, too." He stood up and put his dishes
into the dishwasher.

"I'll be all right here."

"I could call someone to stay with you. Maybe you could
spend the day at Caroline's. Her mom offered. She said you
could help her by filling her new-client folders."

"I'll be fine here," I said. "I could use the quiet."

"Well, okay," he said. "I'll call you before lunchtime, but
you call me before that if you need to. Oh, don't forget you
have a piano lesson this afternoon."

A piano lesson! I groaned.

"I'll cancel it," he said.

"Really?" I asked. "Can you cancel next week's lesson, too? And all of next fall's?"

"Ha ha. Well, you do have that appointment with the therapist, Mr. Thurston, at five-thirty, remember? You don't have to do both. Not this week. I should have called Mrs. Lawrence to reschedule your lesson once we made the therapy appointment."

"Do I have to see a therapist, really?" I didn't want to talk to anyone about what Burgess Newman did. I knew when we made the appointment that that's what it would be about, but, oh, how I didn't want to do that! I didn't want to talk about it or even think about it. "I'd rather cancel the therapy appointment and keep the piano lesson."

"We can't do that," said Pa. "With something as bad as what happened to you—well, therapy is important. I'll call Mrs. Lawrence to cancel, though. She'll understand."

Understand! I didn't even want her to know. Besides, suddenly I wanted that piano lesson. I wanted it even though I'd never really liked studying music. Piano lessons were part of what made my life normal. They seemed set in concrete, and with feeling hot and cold and sore all over, I sure wanted that.

"Don't cancel my piano lesson, Pa," I said. "I want to go."

"Really?" He gave me a sizing-up look.

"Really."

"All right." But something in his face told me he would call Mrs. Lawrence anyway.

So I said real quick, "Please don't tell her what happened. I don't want her looking at me all funny."

After a moment he nodded. "Sure, sugar," he said. "I understand." He hesitated, though, gazing at me like he wanted to tell me something but didn't know how.

"What?" I asked. "What's the matter?"

"Well, Mrs. Lawrence will know something happened," he said.

"Why?" I asked. He was still looking at me, so sad, and I felt a sinking sensation. "Oh, my face. I forgot." I touched the thread ends above my eye. "I wish I could wear a mask. Then no one would have to think anything." Except for wondering about the mask. Why was there always no answer to anything?

"Still don't want me to tell her?" Pa asked.

"I still don't." I made a decision. "I'll tell her myself when I see her."

"All right, honey," he said. "Well, time to get moving."

Then he was gone, leaving the kitchen door swinging behind him.

I stayed where I was, listening to his stride to the front door, listening to the door slam, listening to the car start up in the garage, then listening again to the the car's motor as it pulled past the kitchen window, past the house, onto the street. I listened as it faded . . .

Quiet.

My breath sounded over the refrigerator's hum. Was the house always this quiet?

I lingered in my chair, not wanting to think of what to do next. I pushed syrup over the islands of French toast, turned the French toast pieces over, then turned them back. But I was full.

"Well." My voice was loud in the quiet. "I guess I'm finished here."

I cleaned up, putting my dishes into the dishwasher along with Pa's. I watched the extra syrup drip down, coating the bottom a transparent brown, before closing it up and leaving the kitchen.

I wandered through the downstairs, stopping in the center of the living room.

One of Pa's books caught my eye, and I picked it up. Something about the Civil War and Robert E. Lee. I opened to the place Pa was saving.

My Dear General:
I am much obliged to you for the fine watermelon. I tried to tempt General Long to stay to eat it, but he would not. Can't you come over and dine with us?

What? Watermelons at a time like that? Thank-you notes with a war going on? How weird and ordinary, I thought. More ordinary than ordinary.

I put the book back where I found it. Watermelons. Who gives watermelons as a *gift?* But why not? What got me, though, was all that killing, and they're thinking of *watermelons?* To eat or not to eat *watermelons?* How could they be eating watermelons with a war going on? But I ate my breakfast that morning.

I glanced around the room again. None of the chairs invited me, and I felt all wrong inside. I sat down on the couch, but I couldn't figure out how to sit back, how to sit forward, how to sit at all. I stood up again, rejected by the couch.

I kept thinking how I'd have to explain my appearance to Mrs. Lawrence. Those stitches would get her attention right away.

What will I say? I ran into a door? I fell down the steps? A big kid yanked—NEVER MIND!

An afghan hung off an arm of the couch. I refolded it and put it back. Another glance around the room. *Where can I sit?* I felt that even the carpet didn't like me standing on it, and I wished I could lift my feet from it and float, not touching anything.

Hey! I shouted silently. *I live here! I stand where I want!*

Quiet. So quiet.

"Lalalalaaah," I sang. There. That was better. "Lalalalaaah!" I sighed loudly.

Sound. I needed sound!

I stepped to the piano and ran my fingers over the piano keys. Good! I played a C-major arpeggio. Good!

Without taking my fingers off the keys, I sat down and started my practicing. Loud and louder. GOOD! Teach this house to be so quiet. Ha!

I practiced and practiced, and boy, did I learn all that Mrs. Lawrence had assigned me for the week. And then I practiced some more so the music was like finger painting, moving colors under my hands.

When I finished, the music stayed in my veins, and I felt calm . . . for a while. Then I didn't feel so calm, and I returned to the piano.

Pa called halfway through the day just as he promised. "Everything okay over there?" he asked.

"Just fine," I said. "The house gets kind of quiet, that's all."

"Should I come home?"

"That's all right," I said. "I've been practicing the piano. That helps."

"Well, keep at it," suggested Pa. "I'll be home in a few hours."

We hung up, and I walked around the house again. With

33

thoughts shooting across my brain like hundreds of flying saucers darkening the sky, I looked at the clocks, stared out the windows, sat down, stood up. And every circle I made took me back to the piano, the only place I felt comfortable. It was a new place for that feeling, and it drew me. Practice, circle, practice.

Practicing kept my jumpiness and my fast thoughts from galloping too fast. Practicing. The only thing that would give me peace.

I was still at it when Pa came home.

"This is a first." He beamed at me, obviously pleased.

"I've been playing all day," I said.

"Did you like it?"

"Yes." I was surprised. But it was true. The more I practiced, the more exciting it all was. How had I never known this? I loved it, *and* it saved me.

With Pa's arrival, it was time to leave for my piano lesson. Pa and I went out to the car. I still didn't know what I was going to say to Mrs. Lawrence, and thoughts dashed nonstop through my head.

What will I say to her? What will I say, what will I say?

I had to tell her something, and I couldn't keep a thought nailed down long enough to decide what. Why was my brain acting like this? Slo-o-o-w down.

I'd think of something. Whatever it was, I'd say it and then we'd get into the lesson, and we'd both forget about the cuts on my face.

———

When we arrived at Mrs. Lawrence's house, Pa said, "Do you want me to come in with you?"

"No." I stepped out of the car. "I'll be all right with Mrs. Lawrence. Just wait until I'm inside, okay?"

"Okay. Then I'll make my usual run to the supermarket. We're out of bread again."

"Oh, Pa." I bent to see him through the open car door. "Can you get me some of that great tomato soup at the store's salad bar if they have it? I could eat it between my lesson and the therapy guy."

"In the mood for some tomato, huh?" he asked. "Sure, kiddo."

Then, with Pa sitting in the idling car, I walked toward Mrs. Lawrence's front door. With two minutes left until my lesson time, I still didn't know what to say. I racked my brain for inspiration. I ran into a wall? Fell out of a tree? Fell off my bike? *That one.* I fell off my bike. *Perfect.*

I waved to Pa and entered the house, prepared to wait on Mrs. Lawrence's sofa while she finished up with the kid ahead of me. But Mrs. Lawrence met me at the door, and there was no other kid.

Concern lined her face. "Oh, my dear," she said. "I heard what happened. I'm so sorry. How are you?"

I stared at her, blinking. "How did you know?" I asked.

"I know people who know the Newmans," she said. "But, oh, my dear. How very awful for you. Can I help in any way?"

I hated that anyone had been talking about me, but I said, "That's all right. I'm really okay."

"Are you up to a lesson? We can skip it if you like."

That made me laugh. The one time I wanted my lesson, everybody wanted to let me off the hook.

"No, I really want my lesson," I said.

"Well, then," she said. "Let's go for it."

And boy. I wowed her. After I played through all of my pieces and scales, she sat there for a minute without saying anything.

"That was amazing," she said finally. "You've never played so well."

"I practiced a lot this week," I told her. I didn't want to say *today*. Only *today*.

"I can see that. You practiced hard." There was a pause. "So you like it now, do you?"

"I really do."

"Well, this is very interesting," she said. "I was getting ready to tell your father that maybe we should rethink these lessons."

"Oh, man," I said. "Don't tell him that."

"I won't, now. What a difference." But she looked at me like she knew something I didn't quite know myself.

Then she gave me my week's assignment. There was excitement in her voice that I felt right along with her while she showed me how to approach the new pieces.

As I got ready to go, she held me back. "You've had a rough knock or two this week," she said. "I'm so sorry."

"It's okay." I kept my voice bright. "I just got some cuts that have to heal. That's all. Like when I broke my arm."

"That wasn't any fun, either, was it?" She led me to the front door. "If I can help in any manner, just tell me."

"Piano lessons," I said promptly. "The piano lessons will help."

She smiled in her comfortable way. "I know they will," she said. Then she let me go.

Pa was waiting outside in the car. "Here's your soup," he said.

I took it from him. *"Mmm."* I ate it right up while Pa drove us to the appointment with Mr. Thurston.

5.

Mr. Thurston shared a waiting room with a bunch of other doctors and therapists. I took a seat while Pa told the receptionist we were there. I was wishing I didn't have to be where I was, and that feeling of jumpiness I'd been fighting all day was taking over again. Too bad, I thought, that the piano was at home and I wasn't. I could use a loud playing of a few scales.

Pa took the chair next to mine. "We're a little early," he said.

I nodded, picking up one of the magazines stacked before me on a polished wooden coffee table. I leafed through it, hoping to find a page of jokes or cartoons. Something to distract me, something to keep away the rush of thoughts that zoomed through my head at the speed of light.

Pages and pages of long paragraphs with no beginning and no ending confronted me. Then I found something, a poem with wide empty margins surrounding it.

TO A DAUGHTER WHO WORRIES MUCH
by Eileen Spinelli

Always
I will be your mother,
Long into the spill of time
And when time no longer
Has anything to do with

Dawn or dark.
I will be your mother
Among the oranges,
The local newspapers
And the rattling of cat-bird songs.

You can grow up
Wild and bright.
You can be wind
Or fire,
Willow
Or oak.
You can breathe green.
You can wear poppies
In your hair.
You can stand astonished
In the moonlight
Or peek from a safe,
Moonless space—
I will be your mother.

I may turn into sky
Or red clay
Or simply bones.
I may become delicate
As milkweed
Or hammered hard
As canyon cleft
But I will be
Your mother.

Yes.

Always.

This poem—it said it all. I had to have it.

"Pa," I asked, "do you have any paper on you? I want to copy this."

"Um. Let's see." He pulled a receipt out of his pocket and handed it to me. "Will this do?"

"Sure." And I copied that poem onto the strip of paper as fast as I could. There! Now it was mine.

I put the magazine down and stuck the receipt in my pocket. Pa picked up the magazine and fingered its tattered cover.

"You know," he said, "this magazine's pretty ragged-looking. I bet you could have it if you wanted it. Why don't you ask?"

"Good idea." I'd cut the poem out of the page as soon as we got home and tape it to my dresser mirror. If I could have the magazine.

I stood up and walked to the receptionist, a woman with black hair and bright red lips and a name tag on her blouse. Vivian. She smiled at me.

"Yes?"

"I was wondering." I felt a little nervous on top of my jumpiness.

"Yes?"

"Well, this magazine . . . do you think anyone would care if I kept it?"

I showed Vivian the cover.

"Keep it," she said. "Saves me throwing it out."

I returned to my seat with my new possession.

"Hmm—" said Pa. "So you're a poetry lover."

"This poetry, anyway," I said. "It *means* something."

Pa took the magazine from me and turned to the poem. Before he had time to read it, I heard, "Tracy?"

And there before us was a thin man with glasses and a fringe of gray hair. "I'm Howard Thurston," he said. Pa and I stood up as he extended his hand. I shook it, and Pa shook it, and then we followed Mr. Thurston into one of the offices.

Mr. Thurston was very nice. He was. And I liked him, the way he made sure Pa and I were comfortable in our seats, and the way he talked about how he had a daughter, too, just getting ready for college.

I liked him talking about his daughter. Her name was Debbie, and she made Mr. Thurston crazy the way she drove and sang and talked on the phone, but you could tell he was proud of everything she ever did. Same as Pa was about me.

I looked at Pa, sitting next to me on the two-seater couch, and he was smiling and nodding. Mr. Thurston was smiling and nodding. Maybe I was, too. What was there not to smile about? Debbie was beautiful, Debbie was going to Drexel in the fall, Debbie wouldn't eat pears if you paid her, which Mr. Thurston once tried.

For the first time in two days, I began to relax.

I liked everything about Debbie, especially the part about how she wasn't me and it was she we were talking about. I was happy to let this kind of talk go on forever, and I was wondering if this was how therapy worked. You talked about someone else, and then you felt better about stuff. You didn't have to talk about what made you feel weird.

I wondered how that could work but I was fine with it, and I began to lower my guard and enjoy myself. Mr. Thurston was fun. Anybody'd who'd pay his kid to eat pears had to be fun.

So we were all happy and laughing and talking about Debbie and how she ran marathons, and then Pa was on his feet.

"Hey!" An alarm screamed through me. "Where are you going?"

"Mr. Thurston wants to talk with you alone," Pa said.

I didn't hear that. How did I miss that? What part of the Debbie conversation had Pa leaving the room?

"Is that all right with you?" asked Mr. Thurston. "He can stay if you want."

I looked at Pa. "You'll find it easier to talk without me," he said. "I'll just be in the waiting room. You can call me back anytime."

"All right," I said. As long as that was true. "Don't go far."

"That's my girl," said Pa, and I watched the door close behind him.

Now I didn't like this room so much, and Mr. Thurston's skull looked bumpy and scary through his skin. How could a skull look scary?

"So tell me," said Mr. Thurston, and he still looked friendly and kind even though his skull was scary. But suddenly I didn't like that look, either. I could feel his pity. "Tell me why you're here."

My thoughts began speeding up again. "Didn't Pa say?" I asked. "Didn't he say when he made the appointment?"

"Well, I know what your father said—about a terrible thing that happened." Mr. Thurston's voice was soft. Kind and soft like a ripe peach that you could dent with your thumb without hardly trying. So soft. But I didn't like his soft voice. Scary soft voice to go with his scary skull.

"I don't want to talk about that," I said.

"I understand," he answered. "And you don't have to. The idea here is to try to make you feel more comfortable."

"Good," I said, but I felt uneasy, like a bad thing was going to happen any minute.

"I want to help you get through this."

Through this. Just him saying that felt like someone was pushing the jellylike bruise on my shoulder. Because he was talking about *it.* The thing that happened. We didn't have to talk about it, but just saying that was talking about it and making me see the orangey car and *no-no-no!*

"So," Mr. Thurston asked, "what would you like to talk about?"

I opened my mouth to speak. Nothing came out. After all those galloping thoughts, my mind was blank. I scrambled through the empty space inside my head and found nothing.

"I can't think of anything to say," I said.

"Well, that's all right," he said. "Quiet is okay. Quiet is good." He nodded reassuringly and smiled.

But my mind was anything but quiet. Not quiet, but empty. At least empty where I looked. Noisy everywhere and full of gunky debris that slid away when I tried to see it.

Mr. Thurston sat there looking so concerned, and I hated that. He raised his eyebrows at me, and that made it worse. The steadiness of his scary ripe-peach face while all that gunky debris slithered out of reach made me feel sick.

I wanted to say something, anything to make that scariness leave his face. I searched the corners of my mind. Nothing. I couldn't think; I couldn't remember. Nothing was there. All those thoughts I'd had that wouldn't leave me alone, and now none would hold still long enough to identify.

But wait. There was—oh, no! A picture.

No! I won't look at it.

And a name.

I tried not to hear it. I couldn't not hear it. I shook my head back and forth, back and forth to make the picture and the name go away. Back and forth, back and forth. But they wouldn't go away.

"Tracy? What's wrong?" The softest ripe-peach voice. But with something added to it. Mr. Thurston started to his feet. "Shall I call your father?"

My hands began to shake. "No," I said, but I wasn't answering Mr. Thurston. I would have said yes to his question if I'd heard it right, but the knifelike pain in my gut had all my attention. "No! No!"

I erected a blank wall inside my head. Blank and white and bright and nothing on it. I wouldn't look behind it, or next to it or above it or—I just stared at the center of that bright, blank wall.

But the name. It wouldn't go away.

"Burgess."

I didn't mean to say it out loud, and now it owned the room. How could I get rid of it once it owned the room?

"What? Tracy? I didn't hear that."

Burgess Newman, Burgess Newman, came the surrounding storm. *Burgess Newman, Burgess Newman, Burgess Newman!*

The blank wall teetered—

No, no, nonono, NONO!!

—and fell.

Behind it—*I don't want to see that.* Somebody—a girl—me—being hurt so bad—*nononono!* I was almost crying. Where was the blank, white wall? *Nonononono!*

Burgess Newman!

43

The girl—the girl! Don't do that to the girl!

My stomach heaved and I ran out of Mr. Thurston's office, past Pa in the waiting room to the cold linoleum tiled hallway, where I threw up. On the floor, on the wall, all over me. Why had I eaten that tomato soup?

"Please, let's go," I begged Pa through my heaves. He'd followed me from the waiting room. "Please, please, let's go."

Pa wiped my face and my arms with his handkerchief, nodding, nodding, nodding, with Mr. Thurston standing long-faced in the doorway to the waiting room. He watched while Pa helped me away.

The whole Mr. Thurston thing wasn't as bad as being knocked down by the giant wave, but it was sure bad. And that girl—I hated seeing her like that.

No. No more about the girl. I'm not thinking about it.

Why did I have to see a therapist, anyway? I'd heal on my own without going over what happened on June fifteenth, without thinking about Burgess Newman. I just wanted to go on with my life, and I could do that without help. I was certain of that. I could do the figuring out on my own without telling stuff to *anyone*.

That's what I told Pa between Mr. Thurston's office building and the car. When I wasn't heaving into the bushes.

"Sure, sure," he said. "Listen, you want to just sit on the curb for a minute? Or lie down until your stomach is calm? That would be all right."

"No." I was mostly down to dry heaves, anyway, and I sure didn't want to lie down or sit down anywhere near Mr. Thurston's office. "Just get me out of here." I saw a plastic bag in the gutter and I picked it up for insurance. "Just get me out of here," I repeated before the next bout of heaves had my face buried in the dirty plastic.

Somehow, Pa got me to the car. He put the army blanket we kept in the trunk around me, and that's when I knew I was shivering. How we got home I never knew, but we got there. By that time, the heaving was done, but not the sick feeling. The sick feeling lasted forever.

Pa opened the door on my side of the car. "That was horrible," I said. He pushed the blanket away so it covered the gearshift and the driver's seat, and I stepped onto the driveway with his help. "I never want to do that again."

"Me, neither," Pa agreed.

I went straight from the car to the shower, taking off my clothes in the running water, tossing them from there into the hamper. Oh, the poem! Wet, I stepped out of the shower. I pulled the paper out of my jeans pocket before dropping it onto the bathroom chair. The poem was wet, but at least I had it. What I didn't have was the magazine. I hadn't even remembered it until that second, but at least I had my copy. That was something, anyway. At least I had the poem.

I stepped back into the shower and turned the water on hot and then hotter, but I couldn't take it as hot as I wanted it. I lathered and scrubbed and scrubbed and lathered, and no matter what, it wasn't enough. Finally, I rinsed off and stepped onto the mat. Toweled off.

Still dirty. How was that possible? I looked in the mirror and couldn't see the dirt, but I felt it. It was still there. But how?

Wrapped in the towel, I left the bathroom with the poem in my hand, and before I did anything else, I took some tape from my desk and fixed the poem to my dresser mirror.

Always
I will be your mother,
Long into the spill of time
And when time no longer
Has anything to do with
Dawn or dark.

I stood before the dresser reading and reading that poem.

But I was cold in that damp towel. I turned away from the mirror to put on my pajamas and bathrobe. My quilted one with the purple flowers.

Then I went downstairs.

"Feel any better?" Pa asked.

"A little."

I curled up on the sofa, and Pa covered me with the afghan. That felt so good. He brought me a mug of weak, unsweetened tea with soda crackers and sat beside me.

"I hate tea," I said. "You always bring me tea when I don't feel good, and I hate it."

"Yeah," he answered. "My mother used to bring me tea when I was sick, and I hated it, and you'll probably feed it to your kids in twenty-five years, and they'll hate it too. Long live the Winston dynasty!"

And that made me smile.

Pa patted my back. "You don't have to go back to Mr. Thurston," he said. "Not right away." He pulled me close to him and I put my head on his shoulder.

"Good," I responded, "because I'm not going."

"What happened in there? What did Mr. Thurston say that made all that happen?"

"Nothing," I said. "It wasn't his fault. I just, I don't know. I—I just couldn't deal with it."

"I'm sorry we made the appointment so soon," said Pa. "Maybe I should have known better."

"You couldn't know," I said. "How could anybody know?"

"Later will be a better idea," he said. He ran gentle fingers through my hair. "When you're stronger."

"But for now I don't have to go back, right?" I asked.

"For now."

For now. As far as I was concerned, for now meant *forever*. Because I sure wasn't going back to Mr. Thurston or anybody if I could avoid it.

"You need a little more time to deal with the situation," Pa added. "Give yourself some distance."

I agreed, but I didn't tell him the word *never*. *Never* was I going back to Mr. Thurston or any other therapist. *Never!*

What Pa called a little more time could stretch into eons and eons that melted into forever. And that's when I would go back to Mr. Thurston. At the end of forever. Because Pa would see there was no point in therapists for me. I'd be okay, and he'd see that, and we wouldn't ever have to think about any of this stuff again.

6.

Here's what happened next. I played the piano. That's it.

I played the piano and I practiced the piano and I fooled around at the piano. And when I was there, stroking the keys with my fingers, a white light seemed to fall between me and everything else. I could leave my body and drape myself in music like it was the substance and I was the sound wave. How could I not love that?

I looked forward to my lessons with Mrs. Lawrence, something that hadn't ever been true before. Before, she'd seemed like a stiff old lady who never smiled. Now she smiled and didn't seem so old after all, and sometimes even told me jokes. The piano was *it*.

Which really confused Caroline.

"I thought you hated the piano," she said. We were playing Parcheesi and eating vanilla fudge ice cream one evening after dinner. "You only took lessons because your father wanted you to. That's what you told me."

"I really love it, now," I said. "Maybe I had to grow into it."

Maybe that was it. I certainly understood about music now.

"But that's all you ever do," objected Caroline. "Every time I ask you to take a bike ride or climb Monkey Rock, you say you can't. You say you have to practice. Practice, practice, practice. We haven't been to Monkey Rock *once* since school let out."

"It's important."

"I know it is," she answered. "Oh, you mean the piano. The piano." Her voice growled on the repetition.

"The piano is important to me."

"So's Monkey Rock." Caroline lifted her chin to glare at me. "At least it used to be."

Why didn't she understand? But the piano—what it did for me, draping me in the solidity of sound—how could I explain that? And how could I explain how hard it was for me to sit anywhere besides the piano bench? Of course she couldn't understand. Who could understand?

"Well, at least we have basketball camp coming up," Caroline said. "You, me, and Mayella, same as last year. It'll be a blast."

I grinned at her. "Yeah. Four weeks of the best," I said. "Can you believe Andre Iguodala's coming to our basketball camp?"

"He must like kids," said Caroline.

I thought of the camp schedule. Basketball in the morning and swimming in the afternoon. I smiled, thinking about it.

But even before Caroline and I finished our Parcheesi game, I began to worry about the camp. Sure, Andre Iguodala was coming one of the days and so was the guy they called the Comet, from Temple University. I knew we'd get to really play the game, play hard and sweat and get good at it. I'd looked forward to basketball camp all year. But now, as cool as it all was going to be, I didn't want to go.

Don't want to go? asked a voice inside my head. *What do you mean?*

Anybody could be there, was my answer.

The sound of the ball dribbling against the wood floor came to me, the air in my face as I charged the basket, the *swish!* of the net as the ball sank through. I loved all those things

See? returned that asking voice. *See?*

Yeah, but the people. So many people. How can you be all right with so many people?

The asking voice came back once more without a question. *Pa's already paid. You have to go.*

Did I have to?

After Caroline left, I looked for my father in his study.

"Knock knock!"

He looked up at me over his reading glasses. "Where's Caroline?"

"She went home. . . . Pa?"

"What is it?"

"Well, you know basketball camp starts Monday?"

"I hadn't forgotten. I thought we'd buy you some basketball shoes this weekend."

"Oh. Well, can I get out of it? I know you paid for it and all . . ."

Pa took off his glasses and laid them quietly on his desk. "You don't want to go to camp?" He squinted at me, and it wasn't to help him see me.

"I'd rather spend the time practicing the piano."

"You won't get to see your friends," he said. "They'll be at camp. You could go with them and still practice the piano at night. Then you wouldn't have to be stuck here with me all day. I'm going to be working on the house this summer, you know. It might get pretty lonely for you with me retiling the bathroom and scraping and painting the rest of the place."

"I won't be lonely," I said. "Honest."

He looked away from me and then looked back. "Does it still hurt to walk? Is that the real reason?" He got that tense look around his mouth I minded so much.

"Partly." Which was true.

"Is the main reason you don't want to go because you think

50

your—um—legs will hurt if you do all the basketball things?"

"It's my shoulder, too," I said. I kept my voice even, but Pa was listening hard and watching my face, and I knew he heard how even my voice was and knew I was working to keep it that way. "My shoulder and other stuff."

I shrugged, hoping to distract him with motion, but his eyes stayed on mine.

"Don't, Pa," I pleaded. "It's not so bad as your face is saying it is."

He raised his eyebrows while shaking his head. "Yes, it is. It was a terrible thing that happened to you. And you have to recover from it."

"Well, I thought things would feel better by now. All over. But I don't feel that good, yet, Pa, and that's the truth. I'm sorry."

"I'm sorry, too. But we shouldn't be surprised. It takes time to heal, and it's only been a little while. You're scared, though, too, aren't you?"

"Well, maybe a little. I don't know why because there's nobody to be afraid of now." I shoved down the early panic. "Whatever. I just don't want to go. Please can I stay home?"

"If you're sure that's what you want."

"It's what I want."

"You sure, though? I don't want them to tell me you can't join if you change your mind later. The camp has a waiting list."

"I won't change my mind. Can you get your money back?"

"I'm sure that won't be a problem if I call about it tomorrow."

"Good."

I left him feeling like I'd escaped from a death sentence.

Oh, Tracy, I chided myself. *A death sentence? Basketball camp is hardly a death sentence.*

But then I felt the crowded basketball court, people yelling, players pushing, people taking away the air, and anyone who wanted looking in at us from the hall . . . anyone . . . any . . . one . . .

Forget that, Tracy.

I sat at the piano and stretched my fingers over the keyboard. I thought of the long, velvety hours I'd have in the quiet house. Quiet and safe. Quiet except for the piano. Safe with Pa working on his projects. Safe.

The keys depressed under my fingertips and chords of purple and starlight filled the air.

The next day, a Saturday, Caroline called me on the telephone. "Want to go to a movie with Mayella and me this afternoon?" she asked.

But that would mean going outside, going where people are.

"No," I said. "You go without me."

"My treat," she said. "Come on. Get some popcorny air."

I smiled. "Thanks, Caroline, but I don't think so. You guys come see me afterward."

Then, practicing the piano, I forgot all about Caroline and Mayella. A Chopin nocturne had me cloaked in its magic when a touch to my right ear made me jump and brought me to the reality of the living room and Pa standing beside me. I looked up at him.

"Your friends are here," he said.

"Oh!" I left the piano to meet Caroline and Mayella in the front hall.

They grinned at me.

I grinned back. "How was the movie?"

"Great," said Mayella. "You missed a good one."

"Hey, you want something to eat?" I asked. "Chips or something? Some soda?"

"We can't stay," said Caroline.

"My mom'll be up at Caroline's any second," explained Mayella. "Here." She handed me a box. "We brought you some popcorn."

"Mmm," I said. "Nothing like movie popcorn. Thanks."

"It tastes even better when there's a movie to go with it," said Caroline.

"Next time," I said. "Next time."

"Well, we gotta go," said Caroline. She reached for the doorknob. "Oh." She turned around again. "I almost forgot. What time do you want to get picked up on Monday, Tracy?"

"Monday?" I echoed. "What do you mean?"

"For camp," she said.

Camp! I hadn't told her. Why hadn't I told her? Why hadn't I told Mayella?

"Mom was going to drive the first week, I thought." Caroline frowned, thinking. "Aren't I right about that?"

"Oh," I said, my heart sinking into my stomach. "I'm not going."

"What?" asked Mayella.

"I meant to call you guys," I said. "I'm not going."

"Not going?" Caroline repeated. "Not going where?"

"You're not going to basketball camp?" asked Mayella.

"No."

"Basketball camp is where you're not going?" Caroline stared at me.

"Oh, Caroline, Mayella, I'm sorry. I only decided last night. I should have called you guys right away."

"What are you talking about?" said Caroline. "You're signed up. We all are. You have to go."

"I'm not going." I didn't know how else to put it. I should have called her and Mayella. How could I have forgotten? Without meaning to, I brushed the stitches over my eyebrow and winced.

I saw Caroline take in that wince. "But why?" she asked.

"All those people." I touched the stitches again. *Ouch!* What was wrong with me? I held my hands together at hip level so I wouldn't do it again.

Caroline was looking at me funny. "Don't touch it," she said, "or we'll all have to faint. It turned you good and white there for a second."

"I didn't mean to touch it," I answered.

Mayella wasn't paying attention to eyebrow stuff. "Same number as every year," she said. "It's fun with so many people. You learn more."

"I just don't want to go." My left hand held down my right. I just felt nervous, and I *wanted* to rub my forehead. I always rubbed my forehead when I was nervous, I was realizing. No, not this time. Instead, I allowed myself to scratch the back of my neck. Then I held my right hand down again like a prisoner so it wouldn't just go right to my forehead. I needed one of those big collars vets put on dogs when they're hurt.

"But we planned it," Caroline protested. "That guy from Temple's going to be there, remember? And Andre Iguodala?"

"I don't want to play basketball anymore."

"Not play basketball?" Caroline goggled her eyes at me. "Not play *basketball*? But you're the best one on our team."

I didn't answer.

"What about getting to meet Andre Iguodala?" Mayella's eyes had popped wide open, too. "You have his autograph from that big game your dad took you to. He's cool, you said."

"Come on, guys," I pleaded. "I just can't deal with it this year."

Mayella's head lifted up at that, and she angled her face to look sideways at me.

"But you're great at basketball," said Caroline. "You were the whole team last year. The MVP. You *have* to come to camp."

Mayella tugged on Caroline's arm. "Come on, Caroline, let's go." She spoke to her in an undertone. "Seeya, Tracy."

"You were going to play basketball forever," Caroline went on, "and break the gender gap and join the Sixers. Remember? What about all that?"

Mayella tugged again and opened the door. "Come on, Caroline," she said. "We'll see ya later, Trace."

Caroline shrugged off Mayella's hand. "Wait." She faced me, and I just wanted to run. But where could I run? I was in my own house. "What's the deal?"

"I'm going to play the piano and help Pa paint the house," I said. "That's what I'm going to do."

"Can't you play basketball, too?"

"Maybe she'll do basketball camp next year," Mayella said, and I nodded, appreciating the help. "You still have sore places, don't you, Trace? More than those stitches over your eye."

I blinked at Mayella. How did she know?

"Oh, is that it?" asked Caroline. "Well, why didn't you say so? Of course you can't play if you still hurt." And now her face got that concerned look I hated.

"It's all right," I said. "I'm just not ready is all."

"We'll miss you," said Mayella.

Caroline and Mayella left then. I stood on the porch and watched them leave as warning raindrops made dark circles on the pavement. Then it was pouring, and Caroline and Mayella sprinted up the street away from me.

7.

THAT SUMMER I DIDN'T WANT TO GO ANYWHERE, AND I DIDN'T unless Pa was right there with me. The house was safe and good. Outside was scary.

How, then, was I going to go back to school in the fall? With Pa carrying me piggyback? And was he going to sit in the next desk in all my classes, too?

Nuh-uh.

Just to see, I went out one morning without telling Pa. Just went outside when he was in the basement, went outside with the front door key in my hand, and started up the Third Avenue hill. My plan was to go straight up the hill to Caroline's house. I would knock on her door and go inside when her mom answered. Then I'd call Pa to tell him where I was.

But I only got as far as the mailbox that sat halfway between our safe houses. I looked up at Caroline's house, then turned and looked down at mine. Hers, mine, hers, mine. I pivoted like a weather vane pushed back and forth by a deranged wind. I couldn't go forward, and I couldn't go back. Frozen, I put my hand on the mailbox. I thought of the donkey who starved to death standing exactly halfway between two stacks of hay.

Don't be a donkey, I told myself and kicked myself in the leg. *Go!* But where? Which way? And while I stood there trying to figure out what to do, a black car turned onto Third Avenue from the bottom of the hill. It sped up, then slowed to a fast, jerking stop—right next to me!

I didn't wait. I tore off for home. The house key was pointing forward for the last ten feet, and I unlocked that door and got inside so fast! At the dining room window, I looked up the street toward the mailbox. Some short, gray-haired lady was putting stacks of letters into the box. The lady whose black car slowed to a stop and scared me half to death.

Running home like that was so dumb. *Wasn't it?* But I didn't know the black car belonged to an old lady. Maybe the next car wouldn't. Maybe the next car would—

"Enough!" I said out loud.

"What?" I turned away from the window and saw Pa gazing at me from the foot of the stairs. He balanced a folded stepladder on the carpet beside him. "What's enough?"

"Oh, nothing," I said. "Getting started?"

"I suppose," he said. "It's times like this I remember why I went into teaching. Did you hear the phone ring?"

"No. I was outside for a minute."

"Oh. Well, Lily called. Burgess Newman waived the preliminary hearing."

"So I don't have to go?"

"You don't have to go."

"And he's still in jail?"

"He's still in jail."

"Good."

Pa lifted the ladder and started up the steps with it. "Come up and talk to me," he said.

"Okay." I climbed up behind him. "Want some help?"

"Sure," he answered. "I've got a bunch of scrapers."

So we went after the old yellowish wallpaper in the upstairs hall together.

Scrape scrape scrape.

I liked working side-by-side with Pa, taking off wallpaper older than me. I looked up at Pa and he looked down at me, and it was all good. I wanted to scrape wallpaper forever; that's how good it felt.

But my right shoulder began to throb. At first, I tried to ignore it and scrape anyway. I didn't want to stop just because somebody did something to me. I was working with Pa, and it was good. It's what I wanted to do.

But after a few minutes, I stopped. Just stood there staring at the wallpaper with the scraper in my hand.

Pa quit working, too, and gazed down at me. "What's the matter?" he asked.

"I can't do it," I told him. "It's too hard on my shoulder." I felt so mad, mad and frustrated. "I want to do it," I said. "It just hurts too bad."

"Then stop," said Pa. "No gold medals are ever given out for wallpaper scraping."

"But I want to do it."

"And I want to swim the English Channel."

"You can't swim," I said.

"Yeah." He grinned down at me. "That stops me every time."

I grinned back even though I was still mad.

"Maybe when you get to the painting part I can try again," I said.

"Whatever," he answered. "Just keeping me company once in a while would be good enough."

I was so bugged. I couldn't run up the hill and I couldn't scrape wallpaper. *Whose idea is this?* I shouted silently. I went down the steps with clenched fists and didn't stop until I reached the piano.

But I couldn't practice. My shoulder hurt, and I was just too angry. I played notes here and there with my left hand, playing out my frustration, playing out my anger. Making it up as I went along. After a while, my shoulder hurt less, and I started using both hands. The notes got calmer. I liked the chords I was playing and kept on, kept on. And while I kept on, the poem came into my head, and I played to the words of it. *The* poem.

Always	**A broken chord far down in the bass**
I will be your mother,	**Moving up toward the middle of the keyboard**
Long into the spill of time	**Jagged arpeggios into the treble**
And when time no longer	
Has anything to do with	
Dawn or dark.	**Heavy rumbling with half steps in the bass**
I will be your mother	**Descending stepwise in octaves from middle C in right hand down to F**
Among the oranges,	
The local newspapers	
And the rattling of	
cat-bird songs.	**Both hands in treble with staccato jumps**
You can grow up	
Wild and bright.	**Staccato half steps**
You can be wind	
Or fire,	**Scales from bass to treble**

Willow	
Or oak.	**Loud chords in bass**
You can breathe green.	**Light major arpeggios**
You can wear poppies	
In your hair.	**Soft, close harmonies that move up**
You can stand astonished	**Staccato chord in treble**
In the moonlight	
Or peek from a moonless	
space—	**Close minor tones below middle C**
I will be your mother.	**Descending stepwise octaves from C to F**
I may turn into sky	**Moving toward treble**
Or red clay	**Fuller harmonies**
Or simply bones.	**Quieter, sparser**
I may become delicate	
As milkweed	**Staccato dissonances**
Or hammered hard	
As canyon cleft	**Loud, LOUD! With left hand staying static while right descends**
But I will be your	
mother.	**Ascending stepwise octaves circling A**
Yes.	**Seventh chord**
Always.	**To resolution with a major chord and fade to nothing**

"What was that?"
I turned around. Pa stood in the doorway to the hall.
"Oh, I was making stuff up," I said.
"You make up good stuff," he said. "It got my attention."

"I was thinking of the poem from the magazine, and that's what came out."

"Powerful," said Pa. He turned to go. "I always knew my daughter was a genius."

I banged out a G-major seventh chord: *chank!* And Pa laughed.

I felt better and turned to my actual lesson. I could practice now.

———

That's where I spent the summer. Always at the piano, and no exception. I was there when the mailman delivered the mail, I was there while Pa scraped and painted and retiled, and I was there when Caroline turned up.

Thank goodness for Caroline and her fearlessness. At least Caroline could climb down the hill to my house. And over and over she did.

"You're gonna wear a hole in that piano bench," she said one day. "You'll wear a hole right through it and fall and break your butt."

That was what I always liked about Caroline—she was *Caroline*. Nothing funny, no awkwardness.

But now she looked differently at me. Differently since June fifteenth. Not too much, but like I was fragile or something. I didn't notice it so much at first, but then I saw it all the time. In her eyebrows and in her freckles and in the way her earrings dangled.

My sores started to feel so big when she was in the room with me, pretending not to see them. Even after they'd faded and the stitches were gone and places didn't hurt so much anymore. But then she'd smile at me, and her face would return to *almost* the way she looked before Burgess Newman—before Burgess Newman—well, before.

Something wasn't the same, but I couldn't quite put my finger on what it was. Whatever it was, it made me feel like Caroline and I weren't really together the way we used to be. What it was, I came to realize, because I saw the look on everybody's face—the mailman, Mayella, the lady at the checkout counter when I shopped with Pa at the supermarket—it was pity. On all those faces. How come all those people knew to pity me? Not everybody knew. How could everybody know? And yet, the pity was everywhere.

There were two places I didn't see it. One place was on Pa's face.

Sometimes he'd forget and so would I, and we'd have fun just joking around while cleaning up from dinner or reading the Sunday comics. Then another look, a heavy look, would spread over his face—not the Caroline-pity look. It was different from everyone else's.

"Cut it out," I told him once when he was just looking at me from his chair in the living room. He'd been reading and I'd been doing a crossword puzzle on the couch. "I'm not going to fall apart."

"I'm sorry," he said. "I keep remembering what you looked like in the emergency room. It frightens me what that boy did to you. You could have died."

"Well, I didn't, Pa, so cut it out. Stop thinking about it. I never think about it."

"Really?"

"Really. Who wants to think about stuff like that?"

And then we were okay again for a little while.

The only other person who didn't give me the Caroline-pity look was Mrs. Lawrence. I mean, sometimes, she'd look concerned.

"How are your sores doing?" she asked a couple of times. She didn't mind being direct about it, and I liked that.

"Mending," was always my reply, just as direct.

And then we'd get down to work. I'd play, and she'd tell me how to play better. Her face was not about pity, and I could work and work hard for her, and it was all about the music.

"Ahhh!" I shrieked in frustration during one lesson. I was sweating and working so hard on Chopin's *Nocturne*. "I just can't get it right."

"You will," she said. She wrote in my lesson book with a clear, calm expression on her face. And then she told me a little more: where to accent, where my right thumb should go and when. "If you want to be an artist, you have to sweat, my dear."

"I'm sweating all right," I said.

"I know. Keep on sweating and you'll get it."

Then I went home feeling like a normal person. Every week it was like that.

But—Caroline. She came over to see me on those hot summer nights. We played Parcheesi and had bowls of ice cream sometimes. Or, we'd watch an old movie or just giggle together over anything, and it was good. Good ol' TracyenCaroline, CarolinenTracy. Just like always. Except for that pity face.

Finally, I had to say something about it.

"I look like what?" she asked. Her eyes were wide. "I'm not pitying you."

"Your face says you are."

Caroline gave me a funny glance. "That's my ice-cream headache," she said. "I ate the ice cream too fast."

"I see that look all the time."

"Maybe it's my thirteen-year-old face," she said. "It took me three years to shed the ten-year-old one. Listen, let's go outside. It's a great night. You've never see so many stars—that's how clear the sky is tonight. And it's not hot. The afternoon rain cooled everything down."

I didn't answer. How could she ask me this? She knew I didn't go outside.

"Come on," she urged. "We'll walk up to school and shoot a few baskets on the lighted courts. Maybe there'll be some people around who'll play a game with us."

"No. I don't like it out there anymore."

"Burgess is in jail," Caroline said.

She said his name! No one said his name around me anymore.

"He is," she insisted. "You're safe out there."

I just stared at her. Saying his name?

"Look," said Caroline. "If you came to visit me and you saw an elephant in my living room, wouldn't you mention it?"

"What are you talking about?"

"Burgess. What he did is in the room with us all the time."

I made a face, like I was tasting something bad. "You don't know. You can't know."

"I know enough," said Caroline. "You won't go outside because of what he did. And he's not even out there. He can't hurt you."

"I feel like I'm going to see him all the time," I told her. "I feel like he's waiting around every corner to catch me, so he can do it again. I stay where he can't get at me."

"But he's not just around the corner. He's in prison. He can't hurt you."

"Somebody else could," I said. "There are probably a million Burgesses out there."

"Tracy!"

"It's true. Anyone out there can hurt you. How do you know which ones won't? *How?*" I looked at her, wishing she could give me a good answer.

"Tracy," she said, "you have to trust the world better than that."

"I did. And look what happened." I touched the carpet next to where I was sitting. "I trust this house," I said. "Inside."

"You can't stay inside the rest of your life."

"I can for the summer," I said. "That's what I'm doing unless Pa is with me. Unless he says I have to go out."

Caroline stared at the carpet where I had touched it. "But what about Monkey Rock?" She looked up at me. "Hardly anybody ever goes there. Why don't we take that hike? We could go tomorrow. Your dad could come, too. We could take the whole day. What do you say?"

I bit my lower lip and released it. "Not tomorrow," I said. "Another day. I really do miss Monkey Rock." I scooped up a spoonful of ice cream and looked at it before stirring it in again with the rest. "I'll go with you. But not tomorrow. Another day. Before school starts I'll go with you to Monkey Rock, okay?"

"You promise?"

"Cross my heart and hope to die."

"Hope to die!" Caroline frowned at me. "Don't say it that way. Just promise."

I laughed, scooping up some more ice cream. "Just a joke," I said. "Just a silly joke."

8.

Toward the end of July, Pa wanted to make another appointment with Mr. Thurston.

"I don't want to go." I paced from where Pa stood in the kitchen to the back door, from the back door to Pa.

"I know."

"Please don't make me go."

"You have to go, Tracy," Pa said. "If you don't . . . well, you don't know. This could cripple you."

"It won't."

"These things can sneak up on you like a cancer," said Pa. "You don't even know you have it, and then one day, it's everywhere."

"This isn't cancer." I paced the kitchen again and just kept pacing. "It's not even an illness."

"You can't just ignore what happened to you."

"Yes, I can. I don't think about it at all. I don't want to."

"Maybe you should."

My nervousness couldn't keep up with the pacing, and my palms began to sweat. I stopped my feet.

"Fine," I said real fast. "I'll go."

I said that so I could make the conversation go away. So the scream I felt growing in my gut wouldn't come out through my mouth. Once I started, I knew I'd never stop. Never.

"Okay," said Pa. He picked up the telephone to made the appointment, but I left the kitchen so I couldn't hear. I left the kitchen to play Brahms on the piano.

Brahms! What a wonderful place to be. A place where there were no Mr. Thurstons. A place where there was nobody. Nobody and no body. Just light and sound and euphoria. A place to lose one's soul, one's mind, one's being. I wished I could carry that place with me. Brahms. The warmest of the warm. My only regret was that I couldn't keep it around me when I wasn't playing.

When it was time to see Mr. Thurston, I would have to leave the Brahms place empty-handed and empty-hearted.

But there were things I could control. First, I wasn't going to eat anything ahead of time. And since I knew what the deal was, I prepared for it. Like for a test at school.

Here's what I said to Mr. Thurston during the appointment Pa set up for me that day.

"I don't want to talk about what happened."

"Then we won't," he said. "How are you feeling?"

"Pretty good," I answered. "I'm really okay."

"So, why are you here?"

"My father wants me to come. I don't need to, but he thinks I do. I'm okay."

"Well," said Mr. Thurston, "as long as you are here, is there anything I can help you with?"

I thought of the bright blank wall. I thought of how I didn't like to go outside. I thought of how I didn't like how people were looking at me anymore. But I couldn't talk about any of it.

"No," I said. "I'm good." I nodded at him. "I'm good."

"Okay," said Mr. Thurston. "That's great." He gave me a bright smile. "Your father tells me that you play the piano."

"That's right."

"My daughter used to play the piano," he said.

"Debbie?"

"Debbie. My wife and I, we went to so many piano recitals. Every spring."

And we talked about piano recitals (they were always on Sunday afternoons) and getting nervous (Debbie used to get pale starting the day before) and how to memorize pieces (Debbie memorized as she practiced).

Mr. Thurston was working very hard to make me comfortable, but I did not get comfortable. I didn't want to get comfortable. I just wanted to leave and not have to think about *it*. The thing we weren't talking about.

Finally, the hour was over, and Mr. Thurston called Pa to come in.

I was so glad to be finished, I almost ran out the door. I passed Pa in the doorway. "See you outside," I said.

I ran through the waiting room and down the hall to the building's exit. *Made it!* I thought. *Made it!* Such relief to be out of that room!

Wait. Now I'm outside. What was I thinking? Outside!

I kept running until I was at the car. I'd lock myself in there, that's what I'd do. Then I'd be safe.

But when I tried the door, it didn't open. The keys. Pa had the keys. Well, of course he had the keys, but that didn't matter. He was right behind me, wasn't he?

No, he wasn't. When I looked, all I saw was the building entrance with nobody coming out. Pa must have gotten stuck talking with Mr. Thurston.

Well, one thing I knew was that I wasn't going back to Mr. Thurston's office for the keys, so I took a seat on a bench near the car. Pa would be right out, I told myself. He'd be outside where I could see him any second.

Anyway, no one was around, and I was fine, here, in the warm sunshiny afternoon. Wasn't I?

I tried to concentrate on that and the soft summery breezes, but what I really wanted was to go home and climb into my bed. My bed. Safe and warm with the quilt tight around me. I wished I could at least get into the car and lock myself in and slouch down so no one could see me.

I looked back at the building. No Pa.

Oh, why hadn't I asked him for the keys? Inside the car would have been safe. Inside the car would have worked all right. *Probably,* I told myself, *you are safe right here. Right here on this bench. Safe enough.* What was safe enough? I stared at a point on the sidewalk. Concrete. Concrete warmed by the sun. I was perfectly safe by the warm concrete. Nobody around but me.

Should I go back inside? With Pa?

I looked back at the building again. What was taking him so long?

I returned my gaze to that concrete point and bored a hole through it with my eyes. A shadow crossed the whiteness, and I looked up.

Burgess Newman.

He stood holding an ice cream cone about four feet away. Right there in front of me. He didn't come close, just stood on the pavement, staring at me. Staring at me and staring at me. Why wasn't he in jail? Why was he here eating ice cream like a regular person and not sitting in jail? Of all places, why did he have to be *here*? I pushed my spine against the bench slats.

"You wrecked my family," Burgess said finally. "All that stuff you said my brother did." *Did* came out two octaves higher than the rest. "You lied."

Roddy. That's who it was. Not Burgess. Roddy. Roddy with that squeaky voice. But was it Roddy? Was Roddy that tall? He turned his head, and I saw the faint scar that ran from the corner of his right eye into his cheek. I remembered the seesaw accident from first grade that caused it. Roddy.

Running feet pounded noisily against the concrete, and Richard Berkowitz turned up next to Roddy. He stopped suddenly, almost falling over when he saw me. Right behind him came Steve DeWitt. Three pals lined up. All with ice cream cones.

"What're you doing, Rod?" asked Steve. Then he saw me. "Oh." Pause. *"Oh."*

The three of them stared at me. "This is the girl," said Richard finally, "isn't she? Isn't this the girl? Tracy Winston? Right?" Like I wasn't a real person with ears and a brain.

They were looking at me in such a way. In that way.

Roddy stepped forward.

"No," I said. I put my hands out. "No, no. Please."

"What's wrong with you?" asked Roddy. He was still holding his ice cream cone. Evil. His ice-cream cone was evil.

"Jeez," said Steve. "She thinks you're going to do it, too."

Roddy stepped forward again.

"Pa!" I screamed. "Pa!" I wanted to run but I couldn't make my legs work.

"You ruined my brother's life," Roddy said. "He was going to go to Cornell. He was going to be a doctor. Aren't you proud of yourself?"

"Stop it," said Richard. "She's scared."

"We're not going to hurt you," said Steve. "You know us. Since kindergarten."

71

I shook my head and screamed. I screamed and screamed.

Richard and Steve stared at me with wide eyes. Wide, sorry eyes. All while Roddy kept shouting, "Aren't you proud of yourself? Aren't you proud of yourself?"

Then Pa was there, running.

"What's going on?" yelled my father. "Are these boys bothering you? Oh, the Newman kid."

Richard and Steve backed away, but Roddy didn't move.

Pa put his arms around me. "You better get going," Pa said to Roddy. "Use some sense."

"It's a free country," Roddy said. He sauntered away, but after a few steps, he ran to where his friends waited half a block farther down.

"Oh, Pa," I cried. "Pa!" I clung to him and clung to him, and he picked me up like I was still in first grade and carried me to the car.

"What did they do?" asked Pa. "What did they say?"

"I thought it was Burgess," I said. "It wasn't Burgess, but at first, I thought it was Burgess. It was Roddy, and he said it was all my fault that Burgess went to jail. He said I wrecked their family."

"Don't believe him," said Pa. "Burgess did what he did, and he admitted it. Roddy wants to believe something else."

"But why's he gotta say something like that? Why's he gotta come that close and talk like that?"

"I don't know, Tracy. I guess that's just the kind of person he is."

We went home after that, and I took a long, hot shower. Afterward, I lay on my bed wrapped in the quilt with my face to the wall. I slowed my breathing down and hoped it would stop, but it kept on and kept on. Why wouldn't it stop? I gave up and just lay there staring at the wallpaper. For a long time.

The doorbell rang downstairs. I didn't care. I didn't move. I stared.

"Hey."

I rolled over. Caroline was in the doorway. She smiled.

"Your father said it was all right if I came up."

I pushed onto my rear and tried to smile back at her. "Did he call you?"

"I confess," said Caroline. "He did." She sat on the bed by my knees. "Are you okay?"

I threw off the quilt. "I'm fine," I said. "I just had to get over running into Roddy. He stinks."

"Well, he isn't here now," said Caroline. "How about we shoot a few hoops in your driveway? Your dad's on the patio cooking something on the grill, and it's really nice outside."

"Well, okay," I said. "As long as Pa's there."

So we shot hoops in the driveway, and everything was fine. Me and Caroline and the smell of barbecuing hamburgers. Which tasted just great when they were ready. After dinner, we played more basketball until Caroline had to go home.

I went with her to the front walk. I could do that because Pa was watching from the porch, and she was there, too.

"Thanks for coming over," I said. "Thanks for making this day feel ordinary and good."

"Hey," said Caroline. "You'd do it for me."

Then she loped on up the hill with that easy stride of hers.

Good ol' Caroline.

For the rest of the week, I thought about Caroline's "emergency" visit while I practiced the piano. Thought about it while I worked out the phrases, trying to make sense of my life and the music at the same time. Practicing those scales, setting the metronome a little faster every two days, working out the details of my life. I was—I was nailing things down with a ball-peen hammer.

Was Caroline just being kind? But what else could it be? She couldn't actually like me anymore.

People didn't like me, really. Not since June fifteenth. How could they? I didn't like me. Dirty and ugly and wrong.

I was different since Burgess Newman had stopped his car next to me. *Burgess Newman!* I wanted him to crack like a piece of ice and shatter. Shatter into pieces the way my life did. I wanted him to crack like a piece of ice and melt and not evaporate, just lie there forgotten, cracked, melted, and alone.

Everybody in the world knew what happened to me that day, and I felt tired of people pitying me, pretending to like me, and acting like they wanted to be my friends. Especially Caroline. Her pretending was harder to take than anybody else's.

All this was swirling in colors of orange and lime when Caroline pushed on the subject of Monkey Rock. Her pushing on the subject made me think again about going outside. Because summer was closing in like a race car speeding to the finish line. Summer wasn't lasting forever, and I was going to have to go to school. There was just no way around that.

Pa had mentioned homeschooling once, but we agreed that he couldn't really work that much with me and still teach school. So that was out.

But how could I go to school or Monkey Rock or any other

place like a normal kid if I couldn't get past the mailbox halfway to Caroline's house?

So I tried it again. Every day while Pa was working on one of the house projects, I left the house. Holding the front door key, I walked to the sidewalk and turned right. The first day, that's as far as I got, on that first square of sidewalk, feeling an orange moon-size ball standing in my way. I turned around, and the moon-size ball rolled against my back until I was inside the house again.

I knew there was no moon-size ball. I knew that it was in my imagination, but I looked out the window anyhow to see if a giant orange ball blocked my way out. It wasn't there. Of course. Of course, it was invisible, too, so how could I know if it was there or not? How did I know it was orange or where it was?

No. It wasn't real.

I laughed at myself for even thinking about it.

"Okay," I said out loud. "Open the door and try it again."

This time, I left the house on the run. My hands sliced the air as I ran, nullifying the moon-size ball ahead of me. I ran. I ran hard, aiming past the mailbox so I wouldn't get stuck at the halfway point again.

I passed the mailbox and kept running all the way up to the stop sign. I circled the sign and ran back down again, speeding up as I passed the mailbox. *Run, run, run! Run, Tracy, run! RUN!!*

Back in the house, lock the door, sit on the hall floor, and get my breath. *I'm okay! I did it!*

The second day, I ran again. I ran to the stop sign and kept going. Made it to the next street. There's where I turned around, feeling like a basketball set down at the top of a hill. Gravity pulled me home.

Lock the door, sit on the hall floor, and get my breath. *Getting there!*

The third day I ran all the way to school. I felt like I'd sneaked around enemy lines to get there. No one was anywhere around to see me. *I fooled you!* My fingers touched the sun-warmed bricks.

"Tag, you're it," I said. I even laughed, standing there all alone, making a short, secret shadow on the pavement. Then I ran the whole way home. In secret.

Lock the door, sit on the floor, get my breath.

Wow, that was pretty good. I'll be able to go to school. I'll be able to walk all the way up there. Alone.

Wait. Alone? You always walk with Caroline.

But that was the idea that had been forming in the orange and lime behind all the rushing thoughts. The idea that had been forming, now grown into a solid. This was it:

I wasn't going to walk to school with Caroline. Not with Caroline and the Caroline-pity. Before school started I was going to end our friendship.

What?

Not be friends with Caroline? Caroline? Caroline who in June threw a rock named Burgess Newman to the bottom of the pond? *Caroline?*

But I couldn't take her pity.

That was it, and for two days, I didn't go outside, didn't run to stretch what I could do. No more Caroline? What would life be like without Caroline? Thinking about that on the afternoon of the second day, I curled up on the couch with the afghan tight around me. No Caroline?

"What's the matter, Tracy?"

I looked up at Pa. I hadn't heard him come into the room. "Nothing," I said. "Why?"

"You were frowning so hard. And I think that afghan has a stranglehold on you."

I pushed a grin across my face and loosened the crocheted wool. "Nothing to report," I said. "Just thinking about stuff."

He turned to leave, but stopped. "You know you have another appointment with Mr. Thurston tomorrow, right?"

"Already?" I sat up and pushed the afghan completely away. "I don't want to go."

"You have to go, Tracy."

"Why? I'm fine. Why should I go?"

"We'll start with that frown I saw when I came in here. Frowns like that require investigation."

"Pa! That's stupid."

"Yup. But you still have to go." Then he did leave, saying as he went, "On to project number thirty-nine."

I stayed on the couch with another frown on my face. Mr. Thurston! What was the point? I couldn't even remember what happened on June fifteenth anymore. Not really. I never thought about it. So I wouldn't have much to say. How can a person talk about something she can't remember?

The next day I posed that very question to Mr. Thurston.

"Well," he answered, "perhaps we should talk about other things."

"Like what?"

"Your father tells me that you had an unpleasant encounter with Roddy Newman and some of his friends when you left here the last time."

I frowned. Why did Pa have to tell him that? "I saw them," I said. "They were eating ice cream. There's an ice cream shop on the next block."

"That's right, there is. A pretty good one, too."

"Yeah. They make their own ice cream."

Mr. Thurston pursed his lips. Then he said, "So tell me about the encounter with Roddy Newman."

I stared at the bright white wall. "I hate that kid."

"Why?"

"He's mean."

"How? Did he do something?"

"No. I don't know."

Mr. Thurston shifted in his chair. "You're working pretty hard not to think about what happened," he said.

"Maybe," I answered. "I don't want to think about any of it."

We went back and forth and back and forth without talking about anything. Finally, the session was over, but before Mr. Thurston let me go, he said, "I want to help you, Tracy. That's why I'm here. Not to make you more miserable."

"I know," I said. "I just don't know how to do this. That's all I can say."

And then he let me go.

———

I mentioned the problem with Mr. Thurston to Caroline over the next night's ice cream and game of gin. Caroline, my best friend. Caroline who I would soon break up with. I tried not to think of it.

"But—" She hesitated. "Don't you want help?"

"I don't need help." I discarded a seven. "I'm an ordinary person. I'm fine."

Caroline picked up my seven and dropped an ace at the same time.

"You're an ordinary person who lived through an awful thing," Caroline said. "You're an ordinary person who can't make herself go outside. You're an ordinary person who wouldn't go to basketball camp, and you're an ordinary person who plays the piano three zillion times longer every day than she ever used to."

I bit my lower lip. "Hey," I said. "Stop pushing me." I discarded another seven.

"Well?"

"It's not as easy as it looks."

"It doesn't look easy," said Caroline. "Don't you ever want to do some of the things you always liked? Playing the piano all the time—come on. You hate the piano." She picked up my discard and put down a three.

"A person can change," I said. "I love the piano now."

"Well, good. You used to love basketball. You used to love long hikes. Did you stop loving those things?"

I didn't answer right away. "I just want to work things out in my own way."

"All right," she said. "I miss you, though. We aren't doing any fun stuff this summer."

I shook the hair off my shoulders. "I guess I don't like to do some of those fun things anymore," I said. "Maybe I'm changing as I get older. But you don't have to hang around me if you don't want to. You sound like you have other things you'd rather do." I tossed down a seven, and she picked it up.

There. I said it. She had the chance to go on her own.

"Oh, you know I'm not going to walk out on you."

"Don't do me any favors."

"Who's doing you a favor? You're my friend." She tilted her head and looked at me. "Besides, you're more fun than anybody else even if you don't go outside. And I do remember you said, *don't let me be alone*. So I'm not letting you be alone."

"I said that?" Of course, I remembered saying it. "Well, I won't hold you to that. I'm okay now."

"All right," she said. "You're the doctor. But I'm here anyway because I'm your friend and you're cool." She picked up my discard and put down hers. She laid down her hand. "Gin." Four sevens and three kings.

I looked at my hand. An ace and two fours.

"What happened to my cards?" I showed my hand to Caroline, and she burst into laughter.

"You're supposed to take a card before you put one down," said Caroline. She giggled some more. "You gave me all those sevens. Did you know that?"

"Really? I was saving sevens, I thought."

"Ha ha. Are you cheating in reverse?"

"Yes," I said. "I felt so sorry for you that I gave you all my cards. Your win was really my win."

She laughed some more and threw her cards at me. I laughed, too, and threw mine at her. Then she grabbed some from the deck and threw them high. I did, too, and in a second, cards flew everywhere while we laughed like a couple of hyenas. Higher and higher we threw, harder and harder we laughed. Oh, man. Caroline was the best.

Caroline. I couldn't remember when she wasn't my friend. But now? I knew we giggled and all that, but when the giggling was over and the cards put away, the truth was still going to be the truth.

She didn't like me anymore. I hated that it was true, but it was true. I knew it was true because it had to be. She pitied me, but she didn't like me. Here's the reason: Nobody could. Nobody, not even Caroline, could like me. Not since June fifteenth.

But Monkey Rock. I'd promised Caroline I'd hike up to Monkey Rock with her. That promise was what got me pushing my distances—what got me so I could go all the way to school.

Besides, I liked Monkey Rock. I liked Caroline. I wanted to go on that hike with her and smell the trees and the wildflowers under the summer sky. I wanted that.

I'd promised Caroline and I was going to keep my promise. Try not to notice all the time that she was barely tolerating me so we could have one last hike before I carved out a solo circle for myself.

I had to do it. Carve out a solo circle so I could go alone and not be always afraid. Even one friend at school—even Caroline—would crack my bright, white wall. It had to be either no friends or no school, and how could it be no school?

I'd promised Caroline about Monkey Rock, and I made another promise, to myself:

Have the hike. Then tell Caroline good-bye.

9.

Monkey Rock.

I bet we'd hiked there a hundred times! What a great place. And the funny thing was, most times we went, we were the only ones there. You'd think we owned it, that and the peace that you got sitting up there looking over all those woods.

Monkey Rock. The day after I promised the hike to Caroline, I went to the piano thinking about the place. I was warming up at the keyboard and thinking about Monkey Rock and how I felt about it, and playing some scales and thinking about Monkey Rock, and then suddenly I was *hearing* Monkey Rock. The notes vibrated in my fingers, and I knew just which keys to play. I played and played until I got it right, and then I pulled some manuscript paper out of the piano bench and wrote it down while the piece was still warm. It took me all day to get it right, but I did it.

I only wrote it down to show Mrs. Lawrence. I didn't need the notes myself, because I knew the music by then. My heart knew it. By heart. That's what they call memorization, knowing something by heart, and now I knew what by heart really meant. Memorization's only half of it, a quarter of it. The part where it's in you—in your heart and soul—that's the part that makes it real.

I happened to have a lesson scheduled for that afternoon, so I took the new piece of sheet music with me when we left, and laid it against the piano's music rack at Mrs. Lawrence's house first thing.

"What's this?" Mrs. Lawrence asked.

"A piece I wrote," I answered. *"Monkey Rock."* I felt nervous and proud all at once. "Do you want to hear it?"

"Of course," was her answer.

I gave Mrs. Lawrence the written-out music so I could stare ahead without looking at it and she could read it without having to lean forward to see. Then I began.

Again, there was Monkey Rock before me. All the shades of green and brown and gray played together. The mists that darkened the rock and the sun columns that brought out the glints of blue worked their way through the composition. Tone clusters and odd intervals and tonics and dominants all intermeshed to paint the piece. All brought up from the earth the same as the physical place. I was there in mind and body.

Then something funny happened. At a certain part of the piece, I felt a sliding sensation, and suddenly everything moved sideways in my musical progression. I took that section and turned it upside down and inside out and backward. I could feel Mrs. Lawrence stiffen next to me while I went off on that unwritten tangent, but the music pulled me that way, and I kept going, exploring, discovering. It was like finding new kinds of chocolate, and each kind led me to the next kind and the next kind until, except for a tiny little strand, it was hardly chocolate at all. Then I returned on that same strand to somehow find the music I'd written. With a huge chord, I entered the last part and finished the piece on a triumphant forte.

The sound died away, and the room became quiet. I waited for Mrs. Lawrence to comment, but she didn't speak for the longest time.

Then finally: "That was fantastic, my dear. Absolutely fantastic!"

"Thank you," I said. "I wrote that today."

"In only one day?" she asked.

I nodded. "It just came to me. I was thinking about a place in the nature center where I like to hike, and the sounds were just there."

"Well, you are certainly blossoming," Mrs. Lawrence said. "Every week you surprise me. You know something? There is a young-composers competition out in Idaho that I know about. You should enter *Monkey Rock*."

She handed the sheet music back to me.

"Enter *Monkey Rock*?" I repeated. "You mean, have other people look at it? Play it?"

"That's the point of a musical piece, just like the point of a play. You don't keep it locked up in your attic after you write it. You share."

"Well, I don't know." I held the music to my chest. "I don't know about strangers hearing it."

"Well, you decide. The deadline isn't until November first, anyway. But I'll tell you what. If you're going to do it, put that cadenza in. That makes the piece shine."

"Cadenza?"

"The part you made up just now. You'd call that a cadenza, taking off with the theme the way you did. Put that in, too. If you can remember it."

"Oh, I remember it," I said.

"In fact, here." She handed me more manuscript paper from a stack sitting on a neaby table. "Write it now. Take the rest of the lesson for that. The cadenza might not stay with you all the way home." She stood up. "Call me if you need anything, but I don't want to distract you." And she left the room.

I picked up a pencil and set to work, still so far into the piece that it was easy to extract the cadenza from my brain. The notes seemed to write themselves. Once in a while, I tested what I wrote on the piano, but mostly, I worked with the pencil.

It took me a while to write all those notes down, but I did it. When I looked up, Pa and Mrs. Lawrence were standing in the studio doorway.

"All finished?" asked Mrs. Lawrence.

I stood up. "All finished."

She took the manuscript from me. "May I enter it for you? I'll make a copy and keep the original."

"I—I guess. I guess it can't hurt." It was only pencil on paper, right? And it would go to Idaho, right? Nobody there knew me. Nobody knew my face or my scars or anything. I'd just be a name on a piece of paper.

"Good." Mrs. Lawrence turned to Pa. "Our Tracy is some composer."

"What did you write?" Pa asked me.

"Something called *Monkey Rock,*" I said. "I'll play it for you when we get home."

Which I did.

"Puts me right there," said Pa from the nearest chair. "Puts me right there."

———

The afternoon of September fourth came clear and cool. I felt the breeze through the dining room window where I waited to see Caroline ride her bike down the hill to my house. It was a beautiful day, and I was afraid to go.

85

I'd promised, and I had to do it. Tomorrow, school was start-ing. Our hike had to be today if we were going to do it at all.

But this would be the end. I kept reminding myself of that. Otherwise, I was so nervous, I wouldn't be able to make myself go. *Just this, Tracy,* I said to myself. *Just this. You can do this last thing.*

The last CarolinenTracy, TracyenCaroline thing. A good thing and a bad thing all at once. A good thing I didn't want to do attached to a bad thing I didn't want to do. Both, I had to do.

I watched, and here came Caroline down the hill, long brown hair flying behind her. She rode right up to the front porch where I met her.

"Are you ready?" she asked. She was pumped, I could tell.

"Listen to something first." I gestured with my head for her to come inside.

She got off her bike and followed me. "What?"

In answer, I sat at the piano.

"Not again!" The eyebrows under her helmet made a straight line as they came together. "Not one more stupid piano note!"

"Please?" I asked. "So you can understand something."

"I don't want to understand anything," she said. "I just want to go to Monkey Rock. You promised. You *promised.*"

"I'm coming," I said. "But listen first. Please?"

Caroline slouched onto the couch. "Oh, all right." She grabbed a throw pillow and bunched it up under her arms. "Go ahead."

"It's called *Monkey Rock,*" I said. She perked up at that. "I wrote it."

I played the whole, entire thing for her, throwing her a glance once in a while to see how she was taking it, to see if she was going to stay mad the whole time. She was still, staring at some place over my head. I don't think she moved the whole time.

I finished the piece and lifted my feet to swivel around on the bench. "Well?" I asked. "Did you like it?"

"Did I like it!" Caroline exclaimed. "I could almost smell Monkey Rock. That was great!"

I left the piano bench and flopped onto the couch beside her. "That's what practicing seven hours a day does for a person," I said.

"Seven hours a day! Are you crazy?"

"Only when I'm not practicing. That's what I want you to understand."

"But, Tracy, seven hours a day!"

"It makes me feel alive," I said.

"Don't you feel alive right now?"

"Sure." I shrugged. "I'm breathing and talking to you, so I must be alive. But playing the piano and writing music make me feel it all the way through. The vibrations of the notes and the conflicts in the chords, the musical lines. They come apart and come together and travel through my blood veins and make my brain sing. Then it lasts for a while after I stop, sort of like a runner's high."

She looked at me sideways. "Your brain sings?" she asked. She thought I was crazy, I could tell that, and maybe I was.

"And sizzles." I grinned at her puzzled look. "You ready for our hike?"

"I'm ready."

We went outside, then got onto our bikes and got going.

Finally! Here we were, riding up Third Avenue. It felt so

good. I'd been missing this all summer! Maybe I was okay outside, after all. Maybe.

"I'm glad you talked me into this," I told Caroline. "It feels good to be out and pushing these pedals. Flying through the September air."

"Yup," she said, "and Monkey Rock is Monkey Rock. The original, I mean, not the music."

But I have the music, I thought. At least I had that.

Caroline and I had been to Monkey Rock so many times, but it was always great: the ride to the nature center; the hike to the hill; the climb, practically straight up. That was part of what was so cool, having to twist our bodies to find toeholds, grabbing onto tree trunks for support. The hike that day was a great one, and I felt so good, I kept up a running monologue that kept Caroline in stitches.

"Hurry." I reached the summit while she was still struggling past what we called the monkey's chin, a rocky outcropping with weeds growing out of it.

She glanced up. "You and your long legs," she said, but I was looking past her shoulder into the valley.

"The monsters are nipping at your butt!"

"What monsters?" she asked, like *Right! Sure. Whatever.* Oh, it was great!

"Well," I said, slowing down my speech, "there's the Loch Ness Mo-o-onster and the Abo-o-ominable Sno-o-owman and the Jer-r-rsey Devil and—"

Caroline was giggling and climbing, and it all felt like CarolinenTracy, TracyenCaroline. Better than best!

"—and they're all about two inches from your butt," I finished in a faster tempo. "They want you for lunch."

"How about Bluebeard?" Caroline puffed. "Is he there, too?"

"Yup, and Long John Silver and a bunch of vampires and—"

Then she reached the top. She looked down with me to see what I was talking about, like it might be real, and I practically had to sit down, that was so funny.

"Vampires? In broad daylight? Where?"

"You just missed them," I said. "They curled up and died and vanished right as you got up here. They hit a sunbeam. See"—I pointed to a column of dust particles encased in a shaft of sunlight—"you can just make out their remains. See?"

Caroline thought that was so funny, she sat so she could pound her fist on her knee while she laughed.

"Yeah," she said finally, "and where are the Jersey Devil and the Loch Ness Monster and the others?"

"Oh." I was offhand. "You should have seen it. The vampires bit them, so they were vampires, too, and they alllll curled up and died because of a sunbeam." I pointed again. "See what I mean?"

"I see," said Caroline. "I think the vampires bit you and did something to your brain. Be careful of that sun or it'll be bye-bye Tracy."

So silly. And just what the day called for.

I sat next to Caroline. "Watch out," I said. "If I'm a vampire, I might bite you! *Rrrh!*" And I took a pretend bite out of the air.

Caroline laughed even harder than before.

This feels like old times. Only better.

Caroline and I stayed on the top of Monkey Rock for our lunch. Quiet and breezy. I'd brought the soda and Caroline brought the cookies, the way we always did it since our families first let us make the hike alone.

So we were up there eating our sandwiches. Mine was peanut butter and strawberry jam, and hers was bologna and cheese with that brownish mustard she liked. The air was clean and smelled of trees, and all we could hear was the rustling of the leaves around us. Perfect.

This hike to Monkey Rock was the best ever. Like we took all our money out of the bank and spent it on one gigantic bowl of whipped cream and chocolate sprinkles. Oh, why couldn't we stay here forever? Why did even this have to end?

As long as we stayed up there, we had the whipped cream. But we couldn't stay. School was starting the next day, and I had to begin the solo circle before that.

After a long silence, I didn't mean to, but I sighed.

"What's the matter?" Caroline asked.

"Oh, school's starting up again. This has to be over now."

"We'll do it again," Caroline said. "There's weekends and weekends and weekends, and before you know it, it will be summer again."

I gave a half smile. Next summer—so far away, it would be forever to get there. "It's different when school's on both sides of a hike," I said. "And we'll change. Next summer we won't feel the same way. We'll be fourteen! *Fourteen!* What we have today is a thirteen-year-old's thing. We can't keep it. Think of all those old teenagers. You never see them in here."

"I guess we're gonna get stupid, then, huh?" Caroline asked.

"Well, something happens to people when they get older that looks stupid from here." I felt a rush of intensity. "I never want to get so I don't want to ride my bike or climb Monkey Rock with you. Look! Look!" I waved my sandwich over the

90

greenness of the woods below. "Just look at what people are too busy to see!"

"And you think we're going to get like that?"

I shook my head. "I don't know. Everybody else does."

"Well," Caroline said, "at least we have today, and we can remember."

I gave Caroline a sudden grin, trying to drop the passion I felt. "The lemonade lady," I said.

"What else? Should I jump off Monkey Rock because school's going to start and we'll be fourteen next spring? Is that such a tragedy?"

"You're right," I said. "Gotta go to school and become useful citizens." I tried to keep my voice light.

"We'll make sure to have those times when we're not so useful, too," Caroline said. "Hiking and stuff."

"Lemonade lady, lemonade lady," I chanted until Caroline grabbed a handful of weeds growing out of the rock and threw it at me. The chant dissolved into giggles that colored our trip back down the outcropping.

We hiked back to our bikes. Everything felt good, and I tried hard not to think how things were about to end. Tried not to think about blood and gashed flesh and death, which is how the immediate future all kept coming at me.

The whole afternoon I'd tried not to think of it, but now it was all right there in front of me.

TracyenCaroline. At least we'd had today.

While Caroline was getting onto her bike, I looked at her, studying her happy face, wishing it could always look like that, wishing this moment could last forever.

She caught me looking at her and paused. "What?" she asked. "Is there mustard on my chin?"

I shook my head. "No. No mustard." I rocked on my toes, rolling my tires forward and back while she got ready to ride.

Well, she was right. At least we had this.

Caroline swung her left leg over her bike and we started toward the parking lot's exit.

"Oh!" Caroline yelped. She braked, and her bike stopped jaggedly.

"What's wrong?" I stopped my bike, too, and then I saw. Caroline's front tire was flat and torn apart by the remains of a broken beer bottle.

"*Morons!*" she yelled. She got off her bike and examined the mess. "Stupid idiot jerky *morons*!" She looked at me. "That was a new tire."

I shook my head. "We'll just walk," I said, and I got off my bike to go on foot alongside her. As we went, I felt worse and worse. I had to break up with her right now. Now! I didn't want to, but what else could I do? But Caroline. *Caroline!*

I wanted to grab her and hold her and not let the next second happen. Stop the clock, stop time, and stay here with our bikes in this permanently frozen moment.

Caroline!

I hardly knew it when my lips started to move. "I can't be your friend anymore." *Did that come out of my mouth? Did it? Did I really say that?*

Caroline's bike stopped so fast, I thought the rear tire would upend over the front. *"What?"* She stared at me.

Once I started it, I couldn't stop. "I'm ending our friendship." I looked down at my bike, which was stopped, too.

A bomb, that's what it was. A bomb that destroyed everything.

"What? Why?"

"You're not my friend, really," I said. "I'm just someone you've been feeling sorry for since June."

"I've never felt like that," said Caroline. "You're my best friend. I hate what happened to you, but, bottom line, you're my friend."

"I'm tired of all the pretending."

"What pretending?" So wide-eyed.

Oh, Caroline, how can you act like you didn't know? You, of all people.

"I've been thinking about it," I said. "Working it out in my head."

"Is this a joke, Tracy? 'Cause it's not funny."

"You know how you always ask me if I want to do something, like take this bike ride?"

"What's wrong with that?" asked Caroline. She rested the seat of her bike on her hip and faced me.

"And how I always say, I don't see why not?"

"You used to say that. Now you say, *I have to practice.* All summer, *I have to practice, I have to practice.* This was our first hike to Monkey Rock since June, do you realize that? *Monkey Rock!* Because you had to practice. Because you wouldn't come outside."

"All right, so I haven't been saying it lately," I admitted, "but now I see why not."

"What's the reason?"

"I've been working things out." Why wasn't she understanding this? Why did I have to keep explaining? How could she not be in tune with me? "I get it now."

"What do you get?" Caroline demanded. "What can you possibly get? I'm your friend. I thought I was your best friend."

"You don't like me," I said. "That's what I get. You only feel sorry for me. I don't want to be part of that."

Caroline looked upset, but I knew she was only upset because I was onto her. She'd be glad once this whole thing was over. No more playacting.

"Of course I like you," said Caroline. "You're not mad 'cause I got a flat, are you? I didn't see the broken bottle, that's all. It could happen to anybody."

"The flat has nothing to do with anything," I said.

"But, Tracy, we just had the greatest hike ever. And you just said you never wanted to get so you didn't want to ride your bike or climb Monkey Rock with me. Didn't you mean that? Didn't you hear what was coming out of your own mouth?"

"Caroline, you're not going to understand."

Caroline's face turned a deep red. "You bet I'm not!"

"I have to do this. We're not talking to each other anymore." My voice kind of wobbled at the end. "Or anything." An octave higher than normal.

"Tra-ceee! Why?"

I shook my head. "I just can't do it. It's too hard." My voice was high and wrong-sounding. Why couldn't I control it? My hands were shaking and I couldn't take it anymore. I had to get out of there! "Good-bye, Caroline." I jumped on my bike and rode away as fast as I could.

"Tracy! *Tracee!*"

I didn't look back. I could hardly see where I was going through my tears. But I couldn't stop or look back. It would have ruined it all.

10.

I WENT STRAIGHT HOME AFTER THAT, GOING FROM THE SHED TO the back door to the steps to bed, all in one straight line. I felt really awful and rolled myself up tight in my quilt. No. It wasn't a straight line. First I waved at Pa in his study, where he was working on school preparation. Because he would have noticed something wrong if I hadn't.

"How was your hike?" he asked.

"Good," I said. "How are you doing here?"

"Getting there."

"Well, I'm going upstairs," I said. "I kind of have a stomach-ache," which was no lie.

"I'll bring you some tea in a bit," he said.

"Don't bother," I said. "Remember? I don't like tea."

"Still, I'll bring you some."

So I went upstairs and rolled up in that quilt and wished myself ten thousand miles away.

School. If it hadn't been for school, none of this would have had to happen. But I had to go. If I told Pa I couldn't do it—well. I'd be seeing Mr. Thurston all the time.

I knew something bad had happened to me in June, and on the surface, I knew what it was, but I couldn't look too hard at it. It was like a sore that didn't hurt if I didn't touch it.

Sores like that get better if you leave them alone, don't they? Sometimes? Please?

Pa did come up later with my tea. He brought a mug for

himself, too, and sat on the edge of my bed sipping from it.

"You're feeling really lousy, aren't you?" he asked. "I can always tell when you're wrapped up like that. Did you and Caroline have a fight?"

"No." I unwound myself enough so I could sit. "Well, maybe a little one."

"Want to tell me about it?"

"No. I'm just not hanging out with her now."

"You'll make up in another day or two."

"Maybe." I wouldn't.

Pa shrugged. "I'm here if you want me."

"I know."

We sat for a minute just drinking our tea.

"I'm making lasagna tonight," Pa said.

"Lasagna?"

"And salad. With that crusty Italian bread you like. Can you eat it or do you want me to wait until tomorrow night? We could just have soup tonight."

"I feel a little better." I took a sip of the bitter liquid. "I can eat."

Pa nodded at me. "So school starts tomorrow."

I made a face.

"Can you do it?" Pa asked.

"Can I do what?"

"Can you go to school?"

I looked at him. *What?*

"Well, you haven't been out of the house much this summer," he said. "We could try some form of homeschooling."

Oh, the homeschooling issue.

"You can't homeschool me," I reminded him. "Not and teach regular school."

"Grammum could come down from New York for a while to help," Pa said. "She offered. She was a teacher, remember."

I *was* tempted. But then . . . Mr. Thurston. And Grammum would be there all the time. The plus would be that I wouldn't have to face the kids at school. *But.* Nobody would leave me alone if I wasn't okay enough to go to school. Nobody being Pa and Mr. Thurston and Grammum. They'd make me keep touching the sore.

No. I had to be alone to heal. Had to.

"I'll go to school," I said to Pa. "But it was nice of Grammum."

"She says the offer's on the table anytime."

"I'm glad to know," I said, "but really, I'm fine."

"Well." He took one last drink from his mug and stood up. "I've got to act like a history teacher a little longer, and then I'll get cracking on that lasagna."

"Okay," I said. "I'll be down soon."

And it was a nice evening. Pa's best dinner and my *Freaky Friday* DVD on the television later. The funniest movie based on the funniest book in the world. So when I went up to bed, we were both laughing. When I went to bed, I thought, *I'm strong. I can do what I have to do.*

_____

The next morning I got up for school just like usual. Washed my face, combed my hair, got dressed, and had breakfast with Pa. All of it felt strange.

Well, I told myself, it shouldn't feel normal. You're doing something new. It will feel normal soon enough. You'll get used to the deal.

Getting my backpack organized and packing my lunch looked ordinary and normal. How I felt wasn't. No one knew that but me, and if I was the only one that knew, well, wasn't that all right?

I wasn't hurting anyone, was I?

My backpack and lunch were ready. I'd put in Steinbeck's *Travels with Charlie* as my insurance book. All I had to do was leave. Leave and head up the Third Avenue hill to school. All I had to do.

But how could I go? I hadn't been to the school building since that day in June—unless I counted the day I touched the bricks in my silly game of secret tag. But that's all it was that day, just a touch when nobody else was around to bother me. Touch! and a fast run back down the hill. Run run run to safety!

This time, I had to go inside the building and act like everything was normal. Normal! No touch and run this time. I had to stay.

If I didn't go, Pa would want to know the reason. And Grammum would come down from New York, and I'd be in talking to Mr. Thurston all the time and everything would be broken and ruined.

Mr. Thurston. Why did he have to be in the picture?

If it hadn't been for him, maybe I would have asked to stay home. And Grammum could have come down, and she might have taught me algebra *and* how to bake pies. Or maybe she would have taught me Italian or built a tree house with me— all things she knew how to do. I thought of Pa's old tree house at Locust Point and how far I could see from up there.

I paused with my backpack, staring out the window, just staring at the possibilities on the bright white wall. A tree house . . .

Homeschooling with Grammum would be cool. Why not say yes? Why not just turn around and say, "Pa, I do want to homeschool with Grammum?" Why not?

Pa put the newspaper down and smiled at me. "You okay to go?" he asked.

"Oh, yeah." I said it with a grin. Since he put it that way. "I'm fine."

Because I knew what was behind the question. June fifteenth. Ugly, disgusting, horrible June fifteenth. Forget the subject of homeschooling. Why did June fifteenth have to lurk behind every thought Pa had about me?

Kuh! I blinked at the sound of Pa's mug making contact with the table.

"Want me to walk you up?" he asked.

I stared at him. "You never walk me up."

"I know, but I wasn't sure if you were going to walk with Caroline since you argued with her."

"Oh, Caroline," I said, like *oh, her.* "I can walk without Caroline. I can walk alone."

"Are you sure you want to be mad at Caroline?" he asked.

"I don't want to talk about it," I said. I was feeling rocky. Go to school without Caroline? Go to school alone? But I had to. That was the whole point, wasn't it? *But don't make me talk about it.*

"All right," said Pa. "It's not so far. And maybe you'll make up with her before the day is out."

"Maybe," I said.

Maybe something would happen. Maybe a miracle would occur.

A miracle. Right. What miracle?

The miracle was that I was carving out a solo circle so I

could survive. The miracle was that I was strong enough to do that. That was the miracle. The miracle was that I was not still in bed wrapped up hot and tight in my quilt.

I blew Pa a kiss. "See ya later, alligator." Same as always.

"In a while, crocodile," he answered. Pa blew a kiss back, same as always, and I left.

Boy. Same as always. Except for being the alonest girl on the planet.

I knew Pa thought that as long as I had Caroline and some other kids, I was okay, that I would ride out the storm with the support of my friends. He thought friends were everything. That's why he made sure to go to his poker game every month at the Allenders' in Newtown Square.

"The gang keeps me sane," he explained to me once. "Poker's just the excuse. Fathers need their friends same as daughters do. And daughters need their fathers to have friends. So we can all breathe other kinds of fresh air."

He was wrong about me needing friends. I didn't need friends. Maybe other people did, and maybe I did once. Now I was more okay without them. My friends were not really friends. Not anymore. I wondered how they could have been my friends once, and what made them so. A little part of me wondered what could make it happen again, but I pushed that part away. No friends. That was the deal.

I closed the red front door of my house and walked away from it. That was hard, but I did it. Then I took the walk to the sidewalk and turned right. All I had in front of me then was a fifteen-minute hike, straight up the Third Avenue hill to where the road dead-ended into the middle school bus loop. Just fifteen minutes of walking, fifteen minutes of putting one foot in front of the other, and I'd be there. Easy.

I sped up as I passed the mailbox. There. I was closer to Caroline's house than to mine. But I had to pass it, not knock on the door. It wasn't a safe house anymore.

Keep going, keep going. On and on to school. You can do it.

Except first I had to pass Caroline's house.

It seemed as though I ought to cross over and knock on her green door like always. What would happen if I did that? But I couldn't. It would undo everything.

What if she came outside right as I got there? What would I do if that happened? I tensed up. She could come out now. Anytime. She had to get to school the same time as I did. So right now she could come out. Or now. Or now.

What if she did? What if?

Would she automatically join me on the sidewalk like she had so many other days? Would we go on to school, chattering away like always, hardly knowing the distance we traveled and being sorry when we had traveled it because we had to stop being ourselves and act like schoolkids? Would we?

I tensed for it.

But when I passed her house, she didn't come out.

Then I kept thinking that she would, that she'd see me ahead of her and run to catch up. But would she? After what I'd said to her in the nature center's parking lot? I hoped she would, but I hoped she wouldn't, too.

I kept on going, and not long after that, when I hit the intersection half a block later, I heard that familiar dry slam. It echoed through the neighborhood. The dry slam that announced the closing of Caroline's green front door. I didn't turn around. Was it Caroline coming out? Did I really know the unique slam of her front door? Couldn't it be anybody's front door?

Caroline's eyes bored holes into my back. Did she hate me? What was she thinking?

Every intersection I came to, I wanted to turn right and turn right again and go home. There was no second right, of course, because of Wentworth Pond, but I sure wanted to go home instead of walk with Caroline's eyes boring holes in my back all the way to school.

Be strong, I told myself. *You can do it.*

I turned up my speed, half running, pretending to myself that I had a reason to get to school quick—a teacher to see, a library book to return from last year. Something that I *had* to do early, that Caroline would understand without being told, so she would know that I wasn't just trying to get away from her.

All I·wanted was to get to school, find my homeroom, and sit down. Once there, I'd be safe. Safe from— Just safe.

Then I was on the sidewalk that lined the bus loop. The school building stared at me, giving me attitude. It looked just the same as it had when my life felt good. How could it act that way? How could it not care?

Shouldn't the red bricks be crumbling? Shouldn't some be falling out of their geometric patterns? Shouldn't the windows be cracked and hanging from their bent frames?

Shouldn't the building say it was sorry?

How could it be the same? How could it be flat and cold against the morning sky, acting like nothing had happened?

A car passed me on the loop, a blue one, and I was glad it wasn't orange.

Only buses on the bus loop, I wanted to tell the driver, but no buses were on the loop yet. Plenty of time for a quick drop-off, even if it was against the rules.

A small pair of ballet slippers attached to the car's antenna caught my eye. I knew that could only be Mayella's mother behind the wheel of that car. Mayella's mother dropping her off.

Mayella came from a family of ballet dancers, including her father. Except Mayella played basketball, too, so that's how we became friends. She could dribble the ball like nobody's business. They made me the MVP of the seventh-grade team, but in practices I could never get the ball away from Mayella. She'd dribble great, then she'd pass to me and I'd shoot. Basket after basket. Because nobody could get the ball away from Mayella.

I stayed where I was, waiting for Mayella to go inside. I didn't want to meet her or say hello to her mother or talk to anybody. I watched the passenger door open, but nobody got out.

Basketball. I could shoot a few hoops right now, get the feeling of the *swish!* back in my arms. That would feel good. Something to make me feel normal again. But you had to do it with other people around. And I couldn't do it right now, anyway, not as school was about to start. Not when I had to find my homeroom and sit down and be safe. But maybe I'd shoot a few hoops at home after school. Maybe. If Pa was outside, too. To make it safe.

Come on, Mayella, get out of the car. What are you waiting for? Get inside so I can go, too.

Finally, Mayella stuck out her legs and got out of the car, but she didn't walk away from it. She stayed there, talking to somebody, talking, talking, talking to somebody in the back, and in between words, taking nibbles on a piece of jelly toast. I could see the purple even from this distance.

Hurry up! my brain screamed at her. *Get inside! Get inside so I can walk the rest of the way myself before Caroline catches up with me.*

Caroline—where is she? She should have passed me by now.

I turned around as a couple of kids brushed me on their way by.

"Hey," said one—Peter Mahoney, a friend from those CPR classes I took at the Y after sixth grade. "How're ya doin', Trace?"

"Fine," I answered. The words felt stiff coming out of my mouth. "Fine."

Peter kept going, like normal. There was no problem he saw, thank goodness. I looked to see if Caroline was somewhere behind me, maybe talking with someone at the street or maybe waiting for me to get out of her way like I was waiting for Mayella. No. No Caroline unless she was crouched behind those azalea bushes across the street. Would she go to that length to avoid me?

I turned back. Mayella was still there, still nibbling, still talking. What was wrong with her? Why didn't she just go inside?

Then the rear door of Mayella's car opened and someone else's legs stuck out. Stuck out and stood up, and it turned into Caroline.

Caroline!

I looked behind me again, half expecting to see her there, too, coming out from behind the azalea bushes. That's where she should have been, back there somewhere. The green door slammed. I heard it.

It wasn't like Caroline had never ridden places with Mayella before. But she hadn't mentioned anything to me about visiting with Mayella when we were hiking up to Monkey Rock.

That was when we were still friends, so the idea of getting together with Mayella must have happened afterward. But a sleepover on a school night? Must have been, but none of us had ever been allowed to do that before.

Caroline and Mayella, they were *still* standing up there yakking into the blue car. *Come on, you guys!*

More and more walkers passed me.

"Hey, Tracy."

"Hiya, Trace."

"Watcha lookin' at, Trace?"

"Out of the way, girl!"

I couldn't wait on that patch of sidewalk forever. All those people arriving, more and more every second. All those people.

I quit.

I turned and jogged around the school, past the basketball hoops, back behind the cafeteria, over by the track, and around to the front again. A school takes longer to run around than you think. Forever to get past the track, but finally, I was back at the entrance.

The car with the ballet slippers was gone, and so were Caroline and Mayella. *Good!*

But *now* the loop was choked with buses. Kids were everywhere, and the noise was *tremendous*! It made me think of pounding surf and the hardness of rocks, and suddenly I was sweaty all over and I couldn't get my breath.

Oh, no! Oh, no!

I had to get inside. I ran, pushing past people, anonymous, unanimous people. I didn't know what they said, if they said, or how they said. All I knew was that I had to get inside. Inside to Miss McGrath's homeroom at the far end of the first hall.

Finally, I was through the entrance. I felt like I *fell* through it. I just ran, ran, ran, all the way down that hall.

"SLOW DOWN!" roared a voice. Mr. Pinkerton, the assistant principal. I didn't look at him, only slowed my legs, but the racing of my heart kept on and on.

With a rushing behind my ears, I entered Miss McGrath's room and went straight to the first row, last desk, and sat down. I put my head on the desktop until the feeling subsided and I didn't feel so sick. I lifted my head and looked around. The room was half filled with kids. Caroline and Mayella were in seats near the front of the room. Janie Perkins had the desk next to mine.

"You okay?" she asked. "You're looking sort of pale."

"I'm all right," I answered. "Thanks."

She might have said more, but I pulled out *Travels with Charley* and began to read. After a minute, I heard my name and looked up. I wasn't sure who said it, but my eyes were locked with Caroline's. I didn't know what to do. If I moved my eyes, I'd cry, if I didn't move my eyes, I'd cry.

Caroline's smile edged uncertainly around her lips.

No, don't smile! Don't make me smile, don't undo what's been done.

Because if she smiled, I knew I'd either laugh or cry, and either way, she'd be right at my desk to joke with me the way we always did before the bell. And we'd be back at the starting gates, and everything would be too scary and I'd start to cry and—

No! Don't smile!

She smiled.

But, George Fritz! That most irritating of all people, George Fritz, threw his baseball cap between us. I blinked, and his whole body was between us doing some kind of stupid dance.

"Rah, rah, rah," he shouted. "School! Yay! I live for this place!" He threw his baseball cap up, and it hit a light.

"Moron." Janie Perkins looked angry. "Go home."

Then George was gone. Caroline was sitting at her desk with her face to the board. The moment was lost. I should have been glad, but I felt sorry.

11.

My routine got easier after a few days, and I began to feel better. Not great, and not really *better*. Just sort of level.

People got the message. That part amazed me—how fast that happened. How quickly my classmates seemed to forget how I used to be part of everything. Now when I stayed by myself, I got shrugs and a questioning look or two, but that was all.

Once I overheard this from a new girl: "What's the matter with her?"

And someone else answering, "She's the girl who—" *whisper-whisper.* "See the red mark over her eye?"

"Oh!"

And they moved away like I was a bad person to be near. *She's the girl who* . . . I was famous.

I carved my circle even closer.

All around, kids went about their lives without me. They didn't need me. They had other people filling in where I might have been. Even Caroline did.

So there I sat, quiet, in some corner or other, reading a book when other kids were talking or fooling around. The reading was a shield between me and everything else. I knew that, and I was glad. And boy, it wasn't so hard to get lost in the words of John Steinbeck. A great escape route.

So it wasn't *so* hard, except I missed Caroline.

That was the main thing about it, missing Caroline. We'd

had fun together. But after June fifteenth, she was pretending. She knew it, and I knew it.

Pretending! I wasn't standing for it anymore.

I was going for the real.

Then one day in the lunchroom, Peter Mahoney, the boy from my old CPR class, tapped me on the shoulder. "What's with you?" he asked.

"Nothing." I kept my book open.

"You don't like people anymore?"

"I want to be alone," I said.

"Why?"

I looked into his dark brown eyes and saw the truth. He knew, same as everybody. He knew about June fifteenth. I looked around the cafeteria. In every eye that looked back at me I saw it: June fifteenth, June fifteenth, June fifteenth. Why did everybody have to know? Why did it have to be the first thing anyone thought about when they thought about me?

Roddy Newman wasn't blabbing. He wasn't even in school anymore, but still, everybody knew.

Roddy, I thought, *it's not your fault. You might as well have stayed here instead of transferring away. It wouldn't have made any difference.*

Even so, I was glad Roddy wasn't around. Roddy, who always looked like he had just eaten salt. I didn't want to see that look, that just-eaten-salt look. I didn't want to remember, didn't want to, didn't want to. I shivered, remembering.

"Please," I said to Peter, and I hugged my sweatshirt closer to me. "I want to be alone."

"Who are you, Greta Garbo?" The old-time movie star. *"I vant to be alone!"*

I turned my face to my book.

"Okay, Greta," Peter said, and I glanced up at his eyes. They looked hurt. He moved away. "Be alone."

That didn't feel good at all. I wanted to call him back and say—but what could I say? That I didn't want to see June fifteenth in his eyes? How could I explain that? And besides, once he knew, he knew. I couldn't peel that away from him. His eyes would always show it. So would his hair and his skin and his freckles.

So I didn't call him back, only watched him leave. The hurt I saw in him made me hurt, too.

That was bad.

But later, I looked at him, and the sadness had left. He was all right again, joking with his friends, going on with his life without me. So it was all right, wasn't it? I had what I wanted. He had what he wanted.

I was free. That was the main thing. I was free to do what I wanted, to think the way I wanted, to be the way I wanted.

All I had to do was figure out what those things were.

———

School moved on in its usual rhythm while I fit the solitary quiet of my small circle within its larger one. Then one day, Mr. Hanover, the music teacher, knocked everything sideways.

Up until then, nothing much had happened in the music room except for getting to watch a video of *The Music Man*. Watch part of the video, talk about what we'd seen, fill out work sheets. Twice a week for four weeks. Then afterward, a couple of classes to practice the opening scene, where everybody talks in rhythm to the motion of a train.

Learning that opening scene was fun. Fun and anonymous. And no pressure.

But then . . .

"All right," said Mr. Hanover. "We've studied *The Music Man*. Time to move on to another project."

"How about watching *South Pacific*?" one person called out.

"*Grease!*" said another. "Let's watch *Grease!*"

"No. *West Side Story!*"

"*Grease!*"

"*West Side Story!*"

"Hold it," said Mr. Hanover. And it took a couple of minutes to get quiet because Mr. Hanover wasn't very good at keeping kids quiet. "Here's the deal. Time for you people to be creative."

"I'm always creative," said Gabe Miller.

"Good," said Mr. Hanover. "That will help when you and your group are writing a musical skit."

The whole class groaned. At least it wasn't just me. Group projects were the pits.

So that was the new assignment. No more watching videos. Time to take our knowledge and write and act in our own short musicals, so said Mr. Hanover. Didn't we see how it was done with *The Music Man*?

"You all know how to read music . . ." Mr. Hanover said. Right. I didn't think any of us could really read music except the band and orchestra kids and me and whoever else took piano lessons. "You all know how to read music and you all know how to write words. So you can do it."

A fifteen-minute skit with four people in each group. A fifteen-minute skit we had to perform. And the kicker was we had to get together to work on it—*outside of school!* I felt uneasy from the beginning, but when Mr. Hanover said that, my palms started to sweat.

What was wrong with Mr. Hanover? Didn't he know anything? Didn't he understand some of us had issues?

"And," he added, "the whole thing is due in six weeks."

"What if I do it on my own?" asked Harry Butler. "I think better if I work by myself."

Hey, maybe—

"Not an option," said Mr. Hanover. He shook his head from side to side while I ground my teeth, hating him. "Not even an option." Then he read off the names for each group.

Mine had me. Gabe. Mayella. Peter.

I was so glad that Caroline wasn't chosen for my group. I think I would have had to run away if she had been. Mayella would be hard enough.

"Okay, people," Mr. Hanover said. "Break up into your groups. You have the rest of the period to organize your ideas."

"Great," said Gabe. "A whole half hour to come up with an idea for a musical."

I'd never even noticed him before, but I stared at Gabe then, wondering how he could say out loud what I was thinking. He caught me staring at him and winked. I dropped my gaze.

But then he pulled his desk over to mine, and Mayella and Peter followed. I saw Caroline in her group across the room with Avi Martin and the Baldwin twins. I felt sorry for Caroline and Avi because Gertrude and Sam always argued.

"Okay," said Peter. "Anybody have any ideas?"

"Three before breakfast," said Gabe. "None since." He knocked on his head. It made a hollow sound.

"Yeah, well," said Peter. "I don't think you had any then, either."

"Maybe breakfast ideas," suggested Mayella. "Then you ate them."

"I didn't eat ideas," said Gabe. "I ate eggs. Four of them."

While they fooled around I decided I had to say something. Say it before anybody else could decide this one important thing.

"Let's meet at my house," I said. "I have a piano."

It felt funny speaking up like that when I lived in such quiet. But I had to make sure that that's what we did. I couldn't risk having to go somewhere else because I knew it just wouldn't work. I wouldn't go. How could I?

But maybe the other kids wouldn't think that mattered—that part about my having a piano. Maybe they all had pianos. Except for Mayella. I knew she didn't have one. I actually didn't think having a piano mattered much to the project, myself. There were pianos we could use at school if we asked. But I hoped it mattered, at least to the other kids, and that they wouldn't guess my real reason. Well, Mayella might guess.

"Do you play it?" asked Gabe. "Do you play the piano?"

"That's all she ever does," said Mayella. Her face was a blank when she said it. Gabe and Peter didn't pick up on any of the hidden vibrations, and I pretended not to know they were there.

"Good," said Gabe. "So you can do the piano-playing part. What else can anybody do?"

"I can dance," offered Mayella, "if you want dancing. Can anybody sing? Somebody's got to sing."

Gabe and Peter looked at each other.

"I promised my grandmother I would never sing," said Gabe. His voice was solemn. "She was on her deathbed when I promised her that."

"You must have an awful voice," said Mayella.

"I do."

"You did not promise that to your grandmother," said Peter. "Forget that excuse, buddy. You're singing. We're all singing. And I know your grandmother. She lives behind me. We're all singing, even you, Gabe. And I don't want to hear any more about grandmothers and promises. We're all singing."

"No," I said.

They looked at me.

"You don't want Gabe to sing?" asked Peter. "Is he really that bad?"

"Yeah," said Gabe. He looked a little hurt. "Am I really that bad?"

"No," I said. "I didn't mean that." Gabe's face cleared. "*I'm* not singing. I'm playing the piano." That was it. I was playing the piano. I wasn't going to talk, I wasn't going to sing or dance or anything. Would the other kids agree?

"Oh," said Peter. "I figured on that. You can't sing if you're playing, can you?"

"I don't want to try," I said.

"Just play loud," said Gabe. "Real loud."

"Ha ha." Mayella pretended to laugh. "Ha ha." Well, maybe she wasn't pretending. I couldn't tell.

They got down to talking about what the skit would be about. I just listened.

"Okay," said Peter. "How about this? We've got a kid who's made of mud. He's slimy."

"That's your part," said Gabe.

"Fine, I don't care."

"So," said Mayella. "Peter won't take baths and we do what we can to get him to bathe."

"No," said Peter. "The kid's not covered with mud. He's made of mud. You can't wash something made of mud."

"He's a walking garden," put in Mayella.

"So he grows carrots and potatoes under his skin," Gabe added.

"And then," said Peter, "the rain comes down."

"And good-bye Charlie," said Mayella.

I couldn't help smiling. That was pretty funny.

We agreed to meet at my house over the weekend. That was the only part that mattered to me. They were coming to my house.

12.

I was nervous and pacing from room to room.

Pa's here, and it's my house, I told myself. *Pa's here. You'll be all right. And after everybody leaves, you can go upstairs and roll yourself up in the quilt. And besides, Pa's here.*

Mayella was the first to appear. We stood around the front hall, all awkward, while we waited for the others.

"Boys," said Mayella. She shook her head. "Boys are always late."

She said it like we were friends still. I didn't correct her.

"Are they?" I asked.

"What is it . . . snips and snails and puppy dogs' tails?" asked Mayella. "That's what does it to them. It makes them late."

"I'll remember that," I said, just to say something. Just to keep the house from going quiet.

But it went quiet, anyway.

"So, um, how have you been?" asked Mayella.

"All right. And you?"

Formal. We were never formal. How could we be formal after all the fun we'd had together? I wanted to ask Mayella that, but I was afraid.

"I'm okay," she said. "I wonder, though, why you don't want friends anymore. Why? You look so lonely."

I shook my head real quick. "I don't want to talk about it."

I kept my voice low, and hoped Pa hadn't heard the question from his study, where he was grading tests.

"My mother says it's because you got hurt. That you're afraid of people now."

I stared at Mayella without answering. What could I say? Did everybody think this?

"She's wrong," I said finally. "I just have to do this. And I don't look lonely. I'm not lonely."

Mayella nodded. "I only know what I see," she said. "But after you do this—whatever it is that you're doing—Caroline and I, we'd be friends with you again."

My heart hurt, Mayella's voice was so kind and sweet. I could feel screams pushing up from the floor, and if they'd made it to the surface, that would have been it. I would have had to climb up to the roof and grab for the moon if at that moment—knock-knock-knock!—the boys hadn't arrived. I opened the door to them.

"Finally," said Mayella. She winked at me. "Snips and snails."

"Hey!" protested Peter.

"What?" asked Gabe at the same time.

"Oh, come on in," I said, and I led the group into the dining room.

I was so glad the boys showed up when they did. Otherwise—I just didn't know what.

Sitting around the dining room table, we stared at one another.

"So what do we do?" asked Mayella. "What's first?"

Peter took a piece of paper out of his pocket. "I wrote something for the skit," he said. "You want to hear it?" He cleared his throat and began.

You remember Frosty
The snowman come to life
Well, Charlie was a boy of mud
Formed with a potter's knife

He was dark and he was moldy
With acorns for his eyes
But still his mother loved him
So loving were her sighs

Poor Charlie, poor Charlie, the boy his mother made of mud!

Mayella and Gabe laughed, and Peter kept going. The further he got into the poem, the more ridiculous it got and the harder Mayella and Gabe laughed.

Peter ended his poem this way:

But then a dark and stormy cloud
Across the sky did blow
It emptied all the rain it held
On all the land below

It gave the garden such a bath
And Charlie bathed also
And all the mud that was the boy
Washed to the ground —oh, no!

Poor Charlie, poor Charlie, the boy his mother made of mud!

Mayella and Gabe laughed for a long time after Peter finished. Peter grinned.

"That is fantastic," said Gabe finally.

"Thanks," said Peter. "Now we have to figure out how to act it out and stuff."

"Plus write dialogue for the whole rest of the skit," said Mayella. "We've got fifteen minutes to fill, remember."

Peter handed me a copy of his poem. "Can you put music to it?"

All three of them looked at me.

I blinked. "You mean me?"

"Well, you're the piano player," he said. "What about it?"

I thought of the *Monkey Rock* piece and about what I'd made up at the piano for The Poem, and I nodded. I guessed I could do it. I would do it. "Okay," I said, "but you can't complain about what it sounds like."

"That's a good rule, anyway," said Mayella. "No complaining. Everybody works and nobody complains."

So I took the mud-boy poem from Peter. "I'll write the music," I said. "I'll have it when we get together next Saturday."

"Super," said Mayella. "Then we'll all sing it, even Gabe."

And then it got all silly, and by the time Peter's mom rang the doorbell, everything felt normal.

After everyone left, I was exhausted. It took so much out of me to have everyone over! I threw myself on the couch and stared at the ceiling. It was fun, though. Fun. I was almost glad the four of us were working on a project together. No, not almost. I was just plain glad.

Pa settled on a hassock and studied me. "You're looking more and more like your mother all the time," he said. "Even the way you're lying there with your arm at that angle. That's what she used to do."

I looked at my arm. It didn't look anything special to me.

"Do you still miss Mama?" I asked.

"Not so much anymore," he answered. "I mean, I wish she was here. But I've gotten used to her being gone. It has been more than ten years. Most things you can get used to in ten years."

I nodded. "It just seems funny that you never talk about her."

"I haven't forgotten her. Ask me anything you want."

I knew he hadn't forgotten her. And I was making him think about her right now with my arm at some familiar angle on the couch.

"Do you remember the story about the mama-mama bear?" I asked. "I only remember the ending: *The wind blew wild and the wind blew free, but the bear cub was safe in the mouth of the mama-mama bear.*"

He smiled. "Arms," he said. *"The wind blew wild and the wind blew free, but the bear cub was safe in the* arms *of the mama-mama bear."* He sang the words, and the melody stirred something buried far down inside my soul. I could almost remember.

I frowned. "I thought it was *mouth*." The tune he sang echoed through my head. Surely there was more.

"Sometimes it was, now that I think of it." He tilted his head as though listening to far away singing. "You and Georgeanne, your mother, would sing the song over and over, and every time you got to that line, she'd stop so you could put in a different word. Toes, fingers, nose, mouth. It was a game. Safe in the earrings of the mama-mama bear." He sang that. "You giggled pretty hard at that one." He laughed, remembering.

It was a game? And a song? And *mouth* wasn't the right word? *I* added it?

But *mouth* felt right. I wanted it to be right.

"How does the whole song go?" I asked.

"Let's see." He rubbed his forehead. Just the way I did sometimes. "You know, I don't remember. It's been a long time. I heard it so many times, you'd think I'd remember how it went. Mostly what I remember is how you used to look up at your mama while she sang it. One of those warm fuzzies you had going." He smiled over my shoulder as though he was seeing it. I looked to see, too, even though I knew he was only looking at a memory

"Well, if you remember, Pa," I said, "teach it to me. I'd like to know the whole thing."

I spent some time during the next few days thinking about Peter's poem and how to put music to it.

Poor Charlie! Poor Charlie! The boy his mother made of mud!

That part, the refrain, was easy. It just wrote itself. Then I thought about the rest of it. Something silly, something colorful. The same for each set of two verses. And changing the accompaniment with a glissando here, an accelerando there.

On Wednesday, when I thought I had it, I sang it to Pa, playing as I sang. By the time I got to the end, Pa was singing the *Poor Charlie*s with me.

"That's really funny," said Pa. "You'll have them rolling in the aisles."

"Well, I didn't write the words," I said.

"That's why it's called a group project," said Pa. "But your music is just as funny as the lyrics."

"You think so?"

"Sure."

"I thought I'd take it to my lesson tonight," I said. "See what Mrs. Lawrence thinks."

"It'll make her laugh."

Turned out Pa was right.

I put the Charlie sheet music on the rack when I sat down at my teacher's piano.

"You must be in Walter Hanover's music class," said Mrs. Lawrence.

"What makes you say that?"

"You're the third eighth grader to come in with this project." She took the new music from the rack and studied it. "Very funny."

"I didn't write the words," I said.

"No, but the music is funny, too," she said. "I can tell just by looking at it."

"Want to hear it?"

"Sure. Tell you what. I'll sing it and you play it." She stood up with the music to "Poor Charlie." "Or do you need to read it?"

"No," I said. "It's in my head."

So I played the introduction, and Mrs. Lawrence came in like she'd been practicing the piece for weeks. That lady could have been on the stage, the way she sang! I could hardly play, she made me laugh so hard!

After the final *Poor Charlie*s, she sat down and we just laughed together for a long time.

"This is just great," she said. "Mr. Hanover's going to have a treat with this one."

"You think so?"

"I know so."

"Well, do you have any suggestions to make it better?" I asked.

And then we got down to brass tacks about some of the harmonies and passing tones. Everything she said made sense, and by the end of the hour, "Poor Charlie" was really great. But it was also the end of the lesson.

"Oh," I said. "We didn't get to my lesson music."

"That's all right," said Mrs. Lawrence. "Every once in a while we can go off on a tangent. It's all about the music, isn't it?"

"Sure," I said, "but I need some help with the Brahms."

"Next week, dear girl. Next week. We'll devote the whole lesson to the great man if you want."

"Okay," I said. "At least this way, I can teach my group the skit music."

"There you go," said Mrs. Lawrence. She laughed.

"What?"

"Just thinking about Charlie washing away with the rain."

So when the group came over on the next Saturday, I taught them the music to the song.

"That's really cool," said Gabe, "but can I make one suggestion?"

"Sure," I said.

"Well, in the refrain part, you always play a loud bunch of notes on *mud*." He sang to explain: *"The boy his mother made of* **Bang***."* He brought his hands down on an air piano on *Bang!*

"Right," I said. "That's a chord."

"Well, can you play another chord just like that right after we sing *mud*? So it's *'The boy his mother made of mud.'* **BANG**!"

"I can."

"Good, so then we'll sing that, and then on your second, um, chord, Mayella and I will throw globs of mud on Peter here."

"Hey!" Peter sat up straight. "No! No way!"

"Oh, come on," said Mayella. "That'll be hilarious."

"No," said Peter. "You're not throwing mud at me."

"Hey," said Gabe. "If I have to sing, you have to put up with mud."

"But—"

"Remember the no-complaining rule," put in Mayella.

Peter looked at me. "What do you say, Tracy?"

I held my hands palms up. "I don't know," I said. "It's funny, but it's also mud. I wouldn't want it thrown on me, either. Plus we'll have to clean it up afterward."

"It's funny, huh?" Peter asked me.

"It is funny," I said. "I'm sorry." And I was.

"Would you laugh, Tracy, if they threw mud at me?" Peter asked. "Would you?"

I stared at the others, not knowing what to say.

"Listen," said Gabe, "if we get Tracy to laugh at *anything,* you can throw mud at *me*."

I turned bright red at that. It was all I could do not to bolt up the stairs.

"You're on," said Peter. "If Tracy laughs, I get to throw mud at Gabe. So, Tracy, you gotta laugh. But no mud in the face, okay?"

So we agreed there would be no mud in the face and that I would laugh. I wondered if I could laugh.

"Mudslinging," said Mayella. "Good old-fashioned mud-slinging. Now, here's what I want you to do with the dancing."

"Us?" asked Gabe. "Dancing?"

"Us?" echoed Peter.

Mayella pulled Peter from his chair and stood him in the middle of the living room. "Just stand there," she said. "Tracy, can you play the first couple of verses, just to give you guys an idea what I'd like us to do."

So I returned to the keyboard and played the music. Mayella danced around Peter, circling and leaping, and then, on the last chord of the refrain, mimed a throw of mud to Peter's chest.

"Cool," said Gabe when she was finished. "That'll work."

"You're going to do it, too," said Mayella. "You'll mirror me."

"What?"

"You'll mirror me. I'll show you the steps; it won't be hard."

"I promised my grandmother—"

"Ohhhh!" We groaned at Gabe's grandmother.

"Listen," said Mayella. "You and Peter are dancing."

"I'm dancing, too?" asked Peter. "You just had me standing there."

"Yeah, but we're all going to dance the refrain. We'll come to a stop, and Gabe and I'll throw mud at you."

"Seems fair," said Gabe, nodding.

"Says your grandmother," said Peter.

"Leave my grandmother out of it."

"If you will."

"Knock knock!" came Pa's voice.

We looked up and there was Pa with Peter's dad and Mayella's mom and Gabe's older sister. In about a minute, it was just Pa and me again. Quiet.

"Well," said Pa, "how did it go?"

I shook my head and smiled. "You wouldn't believe it."

13.

I PLAYED THE BRAHMS PIECE FOR MRS. LAWRENCE AT MY NEXT lesson.

"Wow!" she exclaimed. "You amaze me, Tracy. Every week you bring me a jewel. A great lesson!"

Then she told me some more about the Brahms, another way to phrase, another way to finger, another way to look at it. With every sentence, another barrier to doing it better, to *getting* it, was removed. I felt inspired, and I wished the lesson could go on forever.

Pa was waiting in Mrs. Lawrence's living room when we came out.

"She's wonderful to teach, Mr. Winston," she told him. "She's just flying."

He looked at me so proud. "She fills the house with music," he said.

"I'm sure of that."

"Shouldn't she be hearing from the young-composers competition soon?" Pa asked.

"Soon," said Mrs. Lawrence. "If you win first place," she said, turning to me, "they call you, but the rest of the entrants get letters. That takes longer."

"I'm not going to win anything," I said. "That was my first real try."

"You never know," said my teacher, "but there are always a few really good pieces that come out of this competition. Last year's winner played her piece with the San Francisco Symphony. But that was a concerto."

"Your piece is the best one," said Pa.

"You didn't hear the others," I said.

"Doesn't matter." I felt the warmth of his beaming smile. "I know it's the best."

"Me, too," said Mrs. Lawrence. "Oh, by the way, I have to cancel next week's lesson. I'll be visiting my son in Houston."

Ohhh! Miss a lesson!

"Well, then," said Pa. "We'll see you in two weeks. Have a good time in Houston."

I waved, not trusting my voice. Pa and I left Mrs. Lawrence's house for the car.

I didn't talk all the way home, trying not to cry. A missed lesson! But why did it bother me so much? I'd missed lessons before. So what? Mrs. Lawrence was coming back, wasn't she? She had a right to visit her son in Houston, didn't she?

"What's the matter, Tracy?" asked Pa. We were stopped at a stop sign. "You're looking sad."

"Oh, nothing," I said. "I just don't want to miss a lesson."

"She'll be back," said Pa cheerily.

"I know." I put on a smile for him. He smiled back, and then we eased on through the intersection.

How could I explain I felt as though part of my personal scaffolding was broken, and how I dangled one-handed from a rope? One-handed from a rope on a sinking ship?

Your whole life is propped up by once-a-week piano lessons? I asked myself. *You can't wait an extra week this one time?*

Sure I can, I answered. I pushed that smile even farther across my face. *Sure I can.*

"Your face'll freeze," said Pa.

I jumped and saw Pa watching me. Yellows and reds from the traffic lights in the intersection where we sat reflected across Pa's chest. I put a real smile on my face. "I was thinking about something," I said.

"Maybe you should think about something else," said Pa. "You looked like Dracula with that crazed look on your face. Do you want to bite somebody?"

"No," I said, giving the word two syllables. *Nowuh.* "I don't want to bite anybody." Except Mrs. Lawrence's son in Houston.

Oh, come on, I scolded myself. *Give it a rest.*

There was still the skit rehearsal on Saturday, right? I mean, I wouldn't see Mrs. Lawrence for a little while, but that didn't mean I had to die or anything. Not with the skit rehearsal on Saturday. That would keep the boat from totally sinking. Right?

At home, I ran over the music for the skit and thought about how Gabe and Mayella and Peter were going to dance and how Peter was going to get hit with mud on my loud tonic chords. Things were going to be okay. When I left the keyboard, I felt lighter and cheerier. I mean, really, Mrs. Lawrence could go visit her son without me totally losing it, right? She could go visit her sister in Hawaii or her aunt in Australia. I could take it. A piece of cake.

A piece of cake with the next skit practice only three days away. The boat floated. I floated.

———

The next morning, I entered my homeroom, and there was Mayella leaning on crutches.

"What happened?" I asked.

"It's a sprain," she answered. "I tripped over one of my sister's skates."

"Oh, no," I said.

"It's not too bad," she told me. "I'll be back dancing in another week. Ten days tops. And I hid my sister's skates." She grinned at me. "She isn't going to find them for a long time."

"Where did you hide them?"

She grinned wider. "I hid them in your backyard," she said. "Behind your shed."

"Oh, you did not."

"Go look and see."

I rolled my eyes. "What about the skit?"

"We can have practice without me dancing."

"I guess we could," I said.

"Sure. We'll just make the boys dance."

I smiled. "I'll leave that to you," I said.

So it was still all right. The boat would still float.

———

On Friday after school, I was working on putting music under the skit's dialogue. The other kids hadn't asked me to, but I was getting ideas of how to use music more throughout the assigned fifteen minutes. Incidental music, I called it. After one section was pretty much under control, I called Mayella on the phone.

"Hey," I said, "tell me what you think of this."

I put the cordless where I could talk and play into it at the same time. I played what I'd made up while I recited the opening lines.

"My name is Mother Potter and I have a story to tell . . ."

When I picked up the phone afterward, I could hear Mayella laughing. Someone else was laughing in the background. Caroline. I swallowed and tried not to mind. Caroline. *I wish we were still friends.*

"What do you think, Mayella?" I pretended I didn't know Caroline was with her.

"It's great," said Mayella.

"Then I'll do more," I said.

We talked for another couple of minutes about the skit. I would have talked about other stuff, but Caroline's being over there made me feel strange, so I said, "Well, I gotta go. I'll see you tomorrow."

I hung up the phone and went back to work, ideas for the incidental music crowding my head.

The ringing of the phone interrupted my thoughts, and I wondered if it was Mayella calling back.

I picked up the cordless in time to hear, "It's Fred Darren, Mr. Winston, from the district attorney's office."

The district attorney's office?

I left the cordless on the piano and stepped away from it without listening to another word. I didn't want to hear another word.

The district attorney's office? Why was someone calling from the district attorney's office? Why?

I headed into the kitchen, where Pa was hanging up the extension. He smiled at me.

Why? I thought. Why did someone call from the district attorney's office? Why?

I didn't want to know, but the question wouldn't go away.

"You sounded great at the piano," Pa said. "It's wonderful having so much music in the house."

"I picked up the phone when it rang," I told him. "What did Mr. Darren say?"

Pa raised his eyebrows at me. "Do you really want to know?"

"No. But I won't be able to think about anything else until you tell me."

"All right, punkin," he said. "Burgess Newman has his court appearance on Monday. This is when he will plead."

"But I don't have to go, right, Pa? I don't have to be there."

"No," said Pa. "Only later if he pleads not guilty."

"Oh, Pa, he has to plead guilty. He said he did it. He has to plead guilty."

"Well, Mr. Darren said he probably will, but we know there is no guarantee. We have to be ready for anything."

"Pa, he has to plead guilty."

"We have to wait and see."

"Don't you think he's going to plead guilty?" What I wanted was for Pa to tell me he was sure Burgess Newman would plead guilty. Of course, he would plead guilty.

"I hope so, punkin, I hope so." He put his arms around me. "Let's have apple turnovers tonight instead of dinner. I bought them at the German bakery after school, and they were hot when I got them. They're still warm."

So that's what we did. Apple turnovers and more apple turnovers. And in the living room afterward, we took turns reading chapters of *The Hitchhiker's Guide to the Galaxy* to each other. Pa read them funnier than I did, and after a couple of his chapters, I was just laughing and laughing.

So I was okay by the time I went to bed. Still laughing and

lighthearted over *The Hitchhiker's Guide,* I settled easily into sleep, almost not thinking about Burgess Newman.

———

First thing the next morning, I got a call from Peter. "I can't come over today," he said. "You'll have to do without me."

"Why can't you come?"

"I have strep throat," he said. "You don't want to catch it. But you can practice without me."

"Mayella's got a sprained ankle," I reminded him.

"Well, you can do the dialogue stuff and the singing at least," said Peter. "And we'll get together next week."

"Sure," I said. "Feel better."

"Thanks."

Before I could take my hand off the phone, it rang again.

"Is this Tracy?" A woman's voice.

"Yes," I said.

"This is Amy Miller, Gabe's mother. He asked me to call you."

"What's the matter?"

"He has a fever and his voice is completely gone. He can't make the practice."

"Oh," I said, feeling smaller and smaller. "I'm sorry he's sick. Peter's sick, too. He has strep throat."

"There's a lot going around."

"Well, tell Gabe I hope he feels better soon."

"I will." And she hung up.

Now we were down to Mayella and me. I called her so she wouldn't be mad to find out when she got here that it was only the two of us today. But we could still do it. The boat could still float.

"Hi, Mayella."

"Tracy! I was just going to call you."

"Are you sick, too?"

"Who's sick?"

I told her about Gabe and Peter. "But we can still practice," I said. "Go over the singing and all."

"I know the singing," she said, "and anyway, I have a problem, too."

Oh, man! Everything was going wrong!

"Did you hurt your ankle again?"

"No, it's not that. My mom wants to take me up to New York today."

"To New York?"

"She got free tickets to a show, so we're gonna go and have dinner and see the show and spend the night. Doesn't that sound cool? Caroline's coming, too."

"Caroline, too?" Why did this bother me? Caroline and Mayella could go wherever they wanted. What was it to me? Mrs. Lawrence could go to Houston, Caroline and Mayella could go to New York. It was a free country.

"I'd have asked you, too," said Mayella, "but I know you don't go anywhere, and you and Caroline aren't talking."

I sighed. I wished we were talking.

"That's okay," I said. "Have a good time."

"Sorry about the skit rehearsal," she said, "but this turned out to be a bad weekend all around. We'll practice next week and work twice as hard."

"Sure," I said, "sure. Don't worry about it."

Then she hung up and I felt really alone. No practice, no piano lesson, and Burgess Newman's plea coming up. The boat was definitely not floating now. Down and down and down it went.

I put the phone on its base and turned around. Pa was there. I wasn't all alone. I had Pa. Pa. Thank goodness for Pa.

"What's going on?" he asked me.

"The rehearsal's off," I said. "The boys are sick and Mayella's going to New York."

"So now your afternoon plans are shot," he said.

"They sure are." I tossed myself onto the couch. Pa sat on the hassock opposite me.

"Well, why don't you call Caroline?" he asked. "She'd come over. Shoot a few hoops out back. That would be fun, wouldn't it?"

It sure would be, I thought.

"She's going with Mayella," I said. *And,* I thought, *how could I ask her?*

"You know I'm going to the Allenders' tonight for poker?" Pa asked.

"I know."

"You want me to stay home? Or get someone to stay with you?"

"No." I kind of wanted Pa to stay, but I felt too old to ask for that. "I sure don't need a babysitter."

"Well, why don't you come with me?"

I lifted a corner of my upper lip. "No thanks. Alex always spits at me," I said.

"You could sit right next to me. Learn how to play. Alex won't spit at you if you're right next to me."

"Yes, he will. He's four and a pain."

"Well, I can't disagree with you there."

"I don't want to go, anyhow, Pa." I hugged a throw pillow.

"Poker's boring. I'll be fine here. I'll watch a movie or read *The Grapes of Wrath*. I've just started that one."

"Still into John Steinbeck?"

"He's good."

"Listen, Tracy." Pa looked at me with his head tilted.

I grabbed another pillow and threw it at him. He caught it, but his eyes didn't change. "Stop looking at me that way!"

"So you're fine?" he asked. "You're okay with this plea coming up?"

I didn't answer. I just squeezed the pillow harder.

"Tracy?"

"Pa," I said finally, "I'll be okay. I just don't feel too good right now."

"Then come outside while I rake leaves. It's a beautiful day."

I followed him out and I even shot a few baskets while he raked leaves. He shot some baskets, too. So it was all right. Except that everything felt grayish brown and lousy. Burgess Newman. All I could think about was Burgess Newman. After a certain point, I left Pa in the yard and read in bed, wrapped up in my quilt. I stayed there until Pa called me to the table for dinner.

"Sure you don't want me to stay home?" Pa asked.

I pushed mashed potatoes through the gravy with my fork. "No," I said. "You go without me. I'm going to lie on the couch and watch *Freaky Friday,* and I don't need you to hang around while I do that."

And after Pa left, that is what I did. I watched. I watched it twice, and it wasn't funny. Either time.

Pa was reading the Sunday paper in his bathrobe when I ventured into the living room late the next morning. He looked up at me over his reading glasses. "Well," he said. "Look who decided to join the living."

Everything still felt grayish brown, but I gave Pa a huge smile—boy, I could have been a Broadway star, the way I could act!—and went on into the kitchen for my cereal.

At my place at the table was a magazine. Why was this here? I picked it up while I ate and leafed through it. A bunch of long articles. I tossed it back onto the table and stared at the tattered cover. Why did it look familiar?

I opened it again to look at the table of contents, but that page had been torn out.

Pa opened the kitchen door and came in. "I see you found it," he said.

"What? The magazine?"

"It's been in the car since June," he said. "I saw it under the army blanket in the trunk last night and brought it in."

"Last June?" I squinted at him. June?

"You wanted it," said Pa. "There's a poem you liked."

"Oh." The one I copied out and taped to my mirror. The one that had fallen off the mirror ages ago and landed behind the dresser where I couldn't reach it. I flipped quickly through the pages until I found it.

TO A DAUGHTER WHO WORRIES MUCH
by Eileen Spinelli

Always
I will be your mother,
Long into the spill of time

And when time no longer
Has anything to do with
Dawn or dark.

I will be your mother
Among the oranges,
The local newspapers
And the rattling of cat-bird songs.

You can grow up
Wild and bright.
You can be wind
Or fire,
Willow
Or oak.
You can breathe green.
You can wear poppies
In your hair.
You can stand astonished
In the moonlight
Or peek from a safe,
Moonless space—
I will be your mother.

I may turn into sky
Or red clay
Or simply bones.
I may become delicate
As milkweed
Or hammered hard

As canyon cleft
But I will be
Your mother.

Yes.

Always.

See? I asked myself. *See?*

But I didn't see. Why couldn't I see it anymore?

I felt so bad, not being able to see it. I could hardly eat any of my cereal, but I had to eat it with Pa hovering around, rinsing out the coffeemaker and chopping green peppers in the food processor. It was when he started to whistle that my tears began, and I quickly tossed the rest of my breakfast into the trash so I could put my dishes into the dishwasher and get out of there before Pa saw me crying.

But my tears made it hard to see, and my hands were shaking with the keeping quiet, and I couldn't get the bowl in its spot in the dishwasher. After three tries, I heard the food processor turn off, and Pa's big hand was on my bowl.

"Let go," he said.

So I did, and he placed the bowl where it belonged. I stayed where I was in my purple-flowered robe, staring into the dishwasher.

"All right, little one," he said, "what gives?"

I didn't answer, and I didn't move. I knew if I did, I'd be crying and sobbing and falling all apart.

Pa didn't seem to understand that. He took me by the hand and led me out to the living room couch, where we sat.

"Tracy," he said. He put his arm around my shoulder and drew me close. "Talk to me."

And even though Pa was kind and gentle and all the things a father ought to be, I couldn't talk. I could only shake and cry.

"That's all right," he murmured. "Crying is just fine."

And I wished I could stop because crying made me remember what happened to that other girl. Not the other girl. Me.

Finally, I said to Pa, "I just don't feel right. I'm going back to bed."

Which is where I spent all the rest of the day. I wanted to sleep, but I couldn't. All I could do was cry or stare into space. Pa came to see how I was doing once in a while, bringing me tea and crackers and just sitting with me while he read.

"I think I better call Mr. Thurston," he said one of those times. "I'll call his number right now. See if he can fit you in tomorrow."

I nodded, but I didn't want to see Mr. Thurston. I only wanted to die.

14.

I PUT MY HEAD DOWN ON MY DESKTOP AND HALF LISTENED TO the morning announcements. I felt so weird. No food in my stomach since yesterday's tea and crackers because I'd overslept. I wondered if Pa had put lunch money in my backpack pocket. He'd done that when I'd overslept before. I checked. Five dollars. Oh, thank you, Pa! I could make it until lunchtime.

The bright white wall wouldn't stay clear. Different images popped up one after the other on it: Mr. Thurston, an orangey car with no backseat, Mr. Thurston, the Locust Point wave and my broken arm, an orangey car, Mr. Thurston, an orangey car.

"Go away," I told the car.

"Huh?" Trevor was twisted to look at me from the seat in front of mine. "What did you say?" he asked.

"Nothing," I answered. "Just talking to myself."

"You told yourself to go away?" His eyes were amused. "I'd like to see how that's done."

"Genetics," I said, to make *him* go away with an answer that would do it. "Superior genetics."

"Interesting gene pool you come from," said Trevor, but he left it at that.

Cut it out, I told myself. *No more talking to yourself.*

If only I could get to a piano. The purple and velvet of music that fixed everything.

Music, my refuge. Music.

When I arrived at my first-period class, I pulled out the

spiral-bound manuscript notebook I'd kept in my backpack since I'd started working on the skit music and turned to a blank page.

Other kids write poetry when nothing's going on in class, I told myself. This is poetry, too.

And I started in—seventh chords, ninths and seconds, and clashing dissonances working from two different keys at the same time. I buried myself in the music, keeping half an eye on Mr. Monahan. But even when I wasn't writing, I was thinking of what to write. Purple and velvet. Purple so dark with lace and velvet and so dark it's black, then purple, then a shock of white.

Music, my refuge.

And then, my brain made a funny turn, and I was hearing the music of the mama-mama bear. I was hearing the music and I was hearing the words and writing them down as fast as I could. All while feeling Mama. Mama in her yellow dress and yellow rose against her dark hair and her warmth and love.

I'd found her! I'd found the way!

I wrote and wrote to keep up, to keep Mama with me.

> *The bear cub was lonely, so lonely and cold*
> *Oh, where could her mama-mama be?*
> *Oh, what will I do, oh, how can I live?*
> *So lonely, so cold, and just me—oh, Mama!*
> *So lonely, so cold, and just me*
>
> *Oh, bear cub, my sweet one, the mama-mama said*
> *She picked up her babe from the floor.*
> *You're safe in my arms, my darlingest one*

There's nothing to fear anymore—my sweet one!
There's nothing to fear anymore.

The winds blew wild and the winds blew free
But the bear cub was safe from all care
So safe in the arms of her mama, my darling,
In the arms of the mama-mama bear—so safe!
In the arms of the mama-mama bear

I sat there and held the sound in my head as long as I could. Mama! Right there beside me with her moonbeam scent and yellow rose. Mama! I could feel her arms around me and her breath above my ear, and all things were perfect and safe again.

I looked at the words before me and changed *arms* to *mouth*. *Safe in the mouth of the mama-mama bear.* Mama. Keep holding me, Mama!

The bell rang, but I couldn't move. I didn't dare. Not with Mama just there. Just, just there. If I moved . . .

"What's the matter, Tracy?" called Mr. Monahan.

I blinked at him. *Oh, no. Mama, don't go!* But she was gone.

"Nothing," I said. "Just thinking hard."

"Well, go on," he said. "I don't want you to be late."

I gathered my stuff together and made my way to my next class. Mama was gone, and I couldn't bring her back. Mama.

So shaky. I felt sick to my stomach. All morning I tried, but I couldn't get the music back. I looked at what I'd written, and I couldn't hear it. Not one note. Shaky.

And without the music, I saw Burgess Newman and heard Burgess Newman.

"Not guilty," he said to a judge. He turned to me. "You wrecked my family." He waved an ice cream cone at me. "Aren't you proud of yourself?" Then back to the judge. "Not guilty. Not guilty. Not guilty."

"Tracy Winston!" I started and looked around. I was in social studies. How did I get there? Miss Moyer, the sub, was taking roll. "Tracy Winston!"

"Here," I answered.

I took my pen and wrote big, hard circles in my music notebook. Harder and bigger and all over the page. So hard I ripped the paper, but I didn't care.

Mayella reached across from the seat beside me and put her hand over my pen-moving one. I stopped my hand and looked at her, leaning across the aisle to me.

"What's wrong?" she whispered.

I shrugged. "Tell you later," I said because I couldn't figure out how to tell her in just a couple of words. *Not guilty, not guilty.*

Mayella nodded, and straightened back in her seat. Her face was serious and she kept her eyes on me for a long second.

I'll tell Mayella later, I thought. Her and Caroline. I can tell them, and that will make it better. But I can't tell Caroline. Why did I have to be so mean to Caroline? I want to tell Caroline.

Then I was seeing Caroline's face the way it was after we left Monkey Rock the last time. Her face and how she shouted *Tracee!* after me. *Tracee!* and *Not guilty!* came together in my ears. Over and over they came. Why couldn't I bring back the bright, white wall?

Mama, where are you? Mama!

"We'll be watching a video on Teddy Roosevelt today." Miss Moyer's announcement filtered through my mental noise.

I tried to pay attention, to make the real stuff outgun the imagined. I watched Miss Moyer wheel the television to the front, focusing on the gray metal stand that glinted under the lights. Why did it have to be gray?

"Why?" asked Avi from the front row, echoing my thought. "We're studying about the colonies." But not my thought. He didn't care what color the television stand was.

Yeah, why? I thought, putting energy behind it. Why? Colonies, right? Why? Why Roosevelt? Why gray?

Not guilty, not guilty!

Tracee!

Aren't you proud of yourself?

MAMA!

Miss Moyer shrugged. "Take it up with Mr. Johnson tomorrow," she said. She put the DVD into its slot. "And don't go to sleep. There's a work sheet afterward he's going to grade."

There was a massive groan. But I was glad, glad that Mr. Johnson was out so I could just sit in the dark and be anonymous.

You can make it, I told myself. *You'll be all right. Lunchtime after this, and you can talk to Mayella. You'll talk about the skit, and that will help.*

But you can't talk to Caroline and Caroline will be right there because Mayella and Caroline always hang out together now. And you should apologize to Caroline, and how are you going to do that?

The Teddy Roosevelt DVD and the work sheet led to the bell. Finally, I could leave.

But I couldn't get my backpack off the floor. One of the straps was tangled in my chair legs, and I couldn't get it loose.

"Here."

Two pairs of hands—one lifting the chair, the other lifting the backpack onto my shoulders. Two. Mayella's and Caroline's.

"Thanks," I said. And they were there. There, staring at me with wide eyes. "What?"

"What's wrong?" asked Mayella. "Something's wrong."

"What is it?" asked Caroline.

I looked at Caroline. "Aren't you too mad at me to care?"

"Do we have time for this?" she asked. "Do we have time for this right now?"

So I just said it. "Burgess Newman is pleading today."

"But he'll plead guilty, won't he?" asked Caroline. "You said he admitted what he did."

I shrugged. "He can still plead not guilty if he wants to."

Caroline and Mayella exchanged a glance. Then, "Come on," said Mayella. She took me by the arm. Caroline took my other one. "Let's go have lunch."

I let them lead me out of the classroom. Down the hall, past the exit to the track, and on to the lunchroom, where I didn't want to go. We got to the edge of the room where the colors of the floor tile changed from giant green and yellow checks to two colors of blue.

I didn't care about the floor tile. Just all those people everywhere. Laughing, curly-haired, hoagie-eating people. Loud people. People everywhere and no room to be. Loud and people. People.

Crash! Somebody dropped a tray.

"No," I said. I started to back away, but the hands of my friends were on my arms.

"What?" asked Caroline. "What's wrong?"

"I can't go in there. I—I need air."

I broke loose and walked fast toward the exit.

"Wait!"

But I didn't wait, couldn't wait, and Caroline ran to catch up with me. "I'll come with you," she said. "We'll both come with you."

"No," I said. "I have to be alone."

"But—"

I stopped for a second and looked into Caroline's dark eyes. I couldn't take her caring dark eyes. "Please," I said. "I need to be alone."

"All right," said Caroline. And she looked hurt. Another time of hurting Caroline. I couldn't stand it.

She stood there while I left, while I went through the double doors and on to the outside.

Outside! I squinted with my first step away from the building. Bright, bright sun made the grass inside the track sparkle. The air was almost warm. I looked around. *Outside!* But better than the lunchroom with all those people everywhere. Until they'd start coming out for recess.

Until then, I had the whole place to myself. Except for one of the custodians, who was pulling a trash can on wheels across the field. If it hadn't been for him, I could have just left. I could have gone into the nature center on the far side of the field and sat next to the creek. Who would have known?

The custodian met me on the track. "What are you doing out here already?" he asked. Bill. That was his name. Bill. It was over his shirt pocket like somebody wrote it in cursive with a pen, but it was thread, not ink. Purple thread.

"I guess I got here ahead of everybody," I said. *Why did Bill want his name written in purple over his pocket? But his shirt was old. Probably the threaded name was blue to start with. Or purple. Maybe it—*

"I guess you did," he answered.

Was Bill going to make me go back inside? I sure didn't want to do that. Maybe he would have, but a pickup truck pulled up against the edge of the service drive and stopped.

"Bill!" shouted the driver.

Bill left the trash can where it was and jogged to the pickup.

I wouldn't go into the nature center, anyway. Bill didn't have to worry about that. I didn't break rules, and that was sure a big rule to break. No, one thing I wasn't going to do was go into the nature center.

I began a circle of the track, and with each stride, I stared at the nature center—the nature center with the creek and all the trees and deer, and Monkey Rock way on the other side of it.

I sure wasn't going to go there. I wouldn't do that. Even if I'd wanted to, I couldn't, not with Bill watching me from the pickup truck. Why was he watching me? What did he think I would do? Knock over the trash can? Just because I came out early, I was bad? I guessed that was it.

I walked. What else could I do? *Tramp, tramp, tramp,* one step after the other, *tramp, tramp, tramp.* Maybe the walking would settle my thoughts and I'd start to feel normal and calm. *Tramp, tramp, tramp, tramp, traaammmmmmmp.*

I had a good rhythm going, but then the rest of the eighth

graders wandered out. The air didn't feel quite so good as it had before, and I couldn't keep the right rhythm. All that walking was lost.

A touch-football game started up on the field inside the track, and some other kids began to circle the track in front of me.

No, I wanted to tell them. *Stay off the track. It's mine today.*

I focused hard on the short part of it in front of me, the part I needed to see so I could walk, and pushed all the other kids off of that consciousness. My private space. Okay. Now I was set. *Tramp, tramp, tramp,* looking for the perfect balance, walking toward solidness.

If I walked enough, maybe the shaky feeling would go away. It would go away, and the cadence of the universe would pulsate through me.

Walking.

Walking.

This came back to me:

> The bear cub was lonely, so lonely and cold
> Oh, where could her mama-mama be?
> Oh, what will I do, oh, how can I live?
> So lonely, so cold, and just me—oh, Mama!
> So lonely, so cold, and just me
>
> Oh, bear cub, my sweet one, the mama-mama said
> She picked up her babe from the floor
> You're safe in my arms, my darlingest one
> There's nothing to fear anymore—my sweet one!
> There's nothing to fear anymore

The winds blew wild and the winds blew free
But the bear cub was safe from all care
So safe in the arms of her mama, my darling,
In the arms of the mama-mama bear—so safe!
In the arms of the mama-mama bear

I thought of the song, and I thought of the song, but I couldn't feel it. Numb, numb, like cold lips. It wouldn't go to that soft place and warm me.

Desperation ran from my heart to my fingertips and my toes and to the ends of each hair on my head. Looking for something, anything I could hold on to, I cast my eye over the football players, the kids who stood around on the grass near the bus loop, the other kids on the track, the teachers. Nothing. Nothing. *Nothing* . . .

"Mama," I whispered. "Have I lost you forever?"

And then, The Poem cracked the sky wide open.

Always, it said, and cloaked the bear cub fear with its love.

I will be your mother

Yes. That's how it was. She would always be my mother.

You're safe in my arms my darlingest one

You can grow up
Wild and bright.
You can be wind

The winds blew wild and the winds blew free
But the bear cub was safe

The bear cub was safe!

Or fire,
Willow
Or oak.

Mama! I am fire, I am willow, I am oak.

You can breathe green.
You can wear poppies
In your hair.
You can stand astonished
In the moonlight
Or peek from a safe,
Moonless space—

I choose the safe moonless space, Mama, if you are there.
Oh, Mama!

The bear cub was lonely
So lonely and cold

I will be your mother
I WILL BE YOUR MOTHER

So lonely.

I WILL BE YOUR MOTHER!
I! WILL! BE! YOUR! MOTHER!

I got it. Mama.

She is, was, and always will be my mother, no matter what. All along, that was the important thing.

The poem leads me. I follow, and the arms of the woods embrace me and carry me away. *Safe in the mouth . . .* oh, Mama! Always.

I walked as far as the creek before I put my backpack down, and stre-e-e-tched my arms over my head as high as they would go. The stretch made me go dizzy and blind. I sat on a rock next to the creek with my head between my knees while the grayness thinned to nothing. After it did, I dipped a finger into the creek.

Cold!

Slowly, slowly, so the shock of it wouldn't change my focus, I inched my palm downward until my wrist was surrounded by the cold, clear water. It was beautiful against my skin, and it sang a tune to me that I could almost hear. I pulled my sleeve up as far as it would go, then pushed my arm in the water up to my elbow to let the barriers between water and blood blur, to let the water's chill wash and heal my scars and let the song's notes enter my pores.

Mama, Mama, in the rays of sun, in the air, in the rustle of the leaves.

"Tracy." She whispered in my ear. "Tracy."

Ahh! So good!

When the time felt right, I stood, letting the trickle of creek water drip onto the ground, making dark, wet passages into the earth. The wind pushed my cheek like a kiss, and I went where it pushed me, farther and farther into the woods.

The canopy overhead thickened, and the brush thickened, closing me into its arms. Soon I would be in the arms, in the mouth of the mama-mama bear.

Safe.

15.

MY CHEEK PRESSED AGAINST SOMETHING ROUGH. I SAT UP, BUT saw nothing. It was dark in the mouth of the mama-mama bear.

The feel of leaves and dark and twigs. Dirt on my face.

I'm not in the mouth of the mama-mama bear. My mind a blank, colored only with the bright white sheet of terror. *Where am I? Who am I? What happened to me?*

But, wait. I'm Tracy. I was on the track, walking and walking during lunch, but I left to find Mama . . .

The mama-mama bear. Mama. *Where is she? Didn't I find her?*

Tracy, pay attention.

Pay attention or you're going to die.

I held the rock under my hands as hard as I could, trying to feel, trying to feel. I stared at the cold moonlight that silvered the treetops below me. Silvered and slivered. *Feel, Tracy, feel! Dig that rock into your skin. Feel!*

Moon slivers touched me at the same instant rock pierced my skin, and I knew all I needed to know. Also, I knew that what I had to do was—

SCREAM!

I screamed and screamed and screamed and screamed.

Suddenly voices and light from everywhere.

"Tracy?" someone shouted. "Tracy?"

"Help!"

I felt myself lifted—how—in the mouth—how—

"She's so light!"—a man's voice.

Mama-mama bear! Hold me, hold me! Don't let them—I reached crazily for my safe place— *No, mamamamamama!!!!*

"Okay, get her down. You have her, Claude? Hold her arms. She's wild."

I screamed. "Mama!" And I sobbed for the girl, me, the other girl, the other me, and how he was hurting her—me. "Mama!" My eyes opened. When had I closed them? I saw Caroline. Her eyes were wide and scared. "The other girl," I said to her. "It's the other girl, Caroline. Don't let her be alone."

She nodded. "I won't, Tracy."

I looked around. "Where's Pa?" I asked. "I need Pa."

"Hiya, Trace."

I opened my eyes in the hospital room. There was Pa. His hand was on mine.

"Hi, Pa," I said.

"How do you feel?" He squeezed my hand gently.

"I'm okay. I feel like I was having a nightmare. But it was real."

"It was real all right." He paused. "We found you on Monkey Rock. You were talking about dolls and bears and moonlight."

"I remember the crazy talk. It all made sense then. But not now. Oh, Pa, I'm so sorry."

"We brought you here and found out you were dehydrated," Pa said. "That can disorient a person."

"Was Caroline there? I sort of remember seeing Caroline."

"She was there. Everyone was looking for you."

"What a mess."

"I should have kept you home today," said my father. "I should have figured that out. You had such a bad weekend."

"Everything fell apart," I said. "Knowing all weekend about Burgess Newman's court date made me feel like I was drowning in mud. And all those good things getting canceled at the same time—my piano lesson and the skit practice—I felt like I was falling, and I couldn't find my way. Am I making sense?"

"Perfect sense," said Pa. "I should have stayed home with you Saturday night, and we both should have stayed home today until we heard the news from the courthouse. After your day yesterday, I don't know what I was thinking, letting you go to school. But you seemed all right this morning."

I bit my lower lip. "You've heard about Burgess Newman, haven't you? What's the news?"

"Guilty. Burgess Newman pleaded guilty."

I heaved a huge sigh. Pa sighed, too, and squeezed my hand again. We didn't talk at all for a minute, just thought together.

"So I don't have to go to court at all?" I asked.

"That's right. Unless you want to be there for sentencing."

"No. I don't need to see that." I sighed again. "Pa?"

"Yes?"

"I don't feel like celebrating or anything. Just sort of blah-ish. I mean, I'm glad and all that that it went this way, but I don't feel any great joy."

"Me, neither," said Pa, "but we can move on, I think."

Pa looked so tired.

"I'm sorry," I said. "I'm sorry that I put you through all this."

"Don't be," he said. "You did nothing wrong. Besides, I'm here for you. I'm always here for you. Good days, bad days, and everything in between. We'll get through this together."

I leaned over and kissed Pa's cheek. "You're the best."

"So are you," said Pa. "I love you, Tracy."

"I love you, too."

Pa put his arms around me and gave me a squeeze. It felt good to be against his chest like that. Pa.

He let me go and we looked at each other and smiled.

"Pa?"

"What?"

"Can I get a different therapist? I want to talk to somebody, but not Mr. Thurston. He scares me."

"Sure," said Pa. "We'll find someone else."

16.

"Tell me why you're here," said Toni Garcia.

"Didn't my father tell you?"

It was the same question Mr. Thurston had asked me way back in June, and my answer was the same, too, but it all felt different. *Why?* I looked at Toni. Her dark blue eyes returned my gaze, and I could just feel something. I didn't know what. She understood. Before I said anything more, I knew she understood.

"We have to work with what *you* tell me," she answered.

So I started to talk.

"I was raped." That was as far as I could go.

Toni looked at me, nodding. "That's pretty terrible," she said. "Can you say any more?"

"No. I mean. This is the first time I've used the word. In all this, I haven't said the word."

"Rape?"

I nodded. "And I don't want to say it again."

"I won't make you."

Toni knew. Somehow she knew.

"Listen," Toni said. "Many women deal with some kind of sexual assault in their lives. More than we know because lots of people don't want to talk about it."

I liked how direct Toni was, like Mrs. Lawrence. Just saying stuff straight out.

"I'm one of them," I said.

"Then why are you here?"

I shook my head. "Mostly because my father says I have to be here. I have to get help. He says so."

"And why do you think he's insisting on therapy?"

I didn't answer, not sure what answer she wanted.

"Well, said Toni, "lots of dads don't make their daughters get therapy when a bad thing happens. Or moms. Sometimes because they think they can handle it within the family. Your father's not doing that. Why not?"

"Because . . . it's too big a thing? Maybe?"

"It is pretty big."

"I mean, the guy almost killed me, too. It wasn't just—it wasn't just the other thing. He beat me up and knocked me out. I should be dead. I would be if the guy had had his wish." I shivered, remembering the feel of gravel against my skin. The burning gravel. "It's not just about the—the other thing."

"It never is."

"You understand," I said.

"Yeah. I do." She looked closely at me. "I do. So, mostly you're here because your dad says you have to be. Right?"

"Yes."

"What's the other part?"

"What other part?"

"The part that's why you're here that doesn't have to do with pleasing your father."

"Well, I think I want to come, anyway. Because. Oh, God." The words were coming out in a rush. "Life has just been so awful. I didn't know what to do. Everything has gone wrong. I lost my mother, and—I mean I lost her a long time ago, but. Oh, I mean, I don't like the way I feel. I just don't like the way I feel."

"Well," said Toni, "why should you?"

And I started to cry. Quiet tears, but so many so fast, I couldn't get my breath. Toni pushed a box of tissues my way, and I took one, two, three, four, five of them, and just cried into the whole, white, crumpled pile.

"I'm sorry," I sobbed. "I'm so sorry."

"Crying is fine," said Toni. "Crying is appropriate, in fact."

And she let me cry. For a long time. I think I used most of the tissues in the box. Finally, I calmed down.

"Better?" asked Toni.

I nodded. "Better." But I still felt so cry-ey. I could have kept on for a week. "Now what?"

"I'll help you."

"How can you help? Everybody knows. Everybody who looks at me—it's in their faces. I feel like I have a brand on my face." I touched the red scar on my forehead. "I do."

"A bad thing happened, and it left its mark. If people see it, then they see it. You should not apologize for what that bad person did to you."

"But I want things to be the way they used to be. I want to feel safe again."

"We'll work on that," said Toni. "But the thing about the world seeing your scar and knowing everything about you, that's really only how you see it. If you saw a kid with a scar, would you think very long about how he got it?"

"Well, maybe not. Everybody's got scars."

"Exactly."

"But lots of people do know. I mean about what happened to me."

"Okay. But let's focus on you and not worry about those

other people so much. Let's give you one useful thing you can leave with today."

But I already had more than one useful thing. Because Toni understood. She cared and she understood.

"You need to grieve," she said.

"Grieve? For my mother, you mean?"

"Well, if you need to grieve for her, you need to do that, too. But that's not what I meant. You need to grieve for the loss of yourself. The part of you that was lost with being attacked."

The part where I lost Mama. The part where I stopped feeling safe.

"Grieve for what you have lost."

I nodded, staring into those blue eyes.

"You know," I said, "you have put your finger on the exact thing."

———

I stood outside the school building a few days later and stared at the pattern of bricks around the entrance. The mortar was coming loose in some places, and an old bird's nest stuck out over the frame of the doorway. How was there room for that up there? And how long had that nest been in that spot? All the kids that went in and out of that door every day, and nobody had taken it down? I wondered if anybody'd seen it besides me.

That nest was there. I liked that.

I sat on the bus-loop curb and studied the building, letting my backpack slip down to the concrete. I remembered how the building had looked to me the first day of eighth grade. Like nothing about it had ever changed, like it was the same since it opened twenty years before. It didn't suffer. It just was and would always be.

But today, I saw the bird's nest and the crumbling mortar, and I thought—even this building has marks. Has brands.

No, I told the structure. You don't have to apologize. You don't have to hug me. But maybe you can hold a baby bird or two on your doorsill once in a while. Be a place the parent birds can build a nest and teach their young ones to fly.

Yes, it's all right. And I'm going to be fine.

The curb was getting hard and cold under my rear, and I angled my legs so I could push to my feet.

It was fun hearing about the honorable mention for *Monkey Rock* yesterday, I thought. Maybe I'll write another piano piece about the bird's nest.

Click! The door opened. Then it closed again with no one coming out.

I adjusted my backpack and started pushing up.

Click! The door opened again.

This time, Caroline came out. She didn't see me sitting on the curb. I hadn't talked to her since that stupid, stupid day when I got so mixed up I tried to find my mother at Monkey Rock. So ridiculous! Looking for Mama at Monkey Rock? What was I thinking?

My mother was dead—and yet I'd felt her all those years. I missed her and her comforting presence. A shard of glass that shattered in the gravel. But it couldn't really have shattered, could it? The love between Mama and me was too strong for that.

Mama was dead. I understood that, sure. But in some way,

she didn't die, couldn't have. Otherwise, how could I have felt her all those years? She was still with me.

Nothing can take you away from me, Mama, not death, not rape, not time, nothing. I know that now.

I watched Caroline adjust her backpack over her shoulders and walk toward the street. When she came even with me, she saw me, hesitated, and went on without speaking. I let her. I didn't know what to say.

Were we friends or not? I wanted to be her friend again. But how? If I could figure out how to say things like *I'm sorry* and—well, maybe that was all I had to know how to say.

"I'm sorry," I whispered, but not for Caroline to hear. To see if I could say the words. "I'm sorry, Caroline. Caroline, I'm sorry. Caroline, I miss you."

I watched her walk across the street and head on down Third Avenue.

"So run after her, you idiot." I hadn't heard any other footsteps, but there was Gabe Miller on my right. He shoved my shoulder. "Go apologize."

"What are you talking about?" I asked.

"Oh, go!" He shoved me again. "You and Caroline. You're friends. Everybody knows it. You know it. So run after her and say you're sorry so you can start acting like it again. What have you got to lose?"

I stood up. "She might not want to be my friend anymore. She may not let me apologize."

"Yeah. Or she might." Gabe put his hands on his hips and gave me a sideways squint. "Do you want me to come with you?"

"*No!*" He took my arm and started to pull. "All right, I'm going! I'm going!"

He let go, and I ran. It felt good to run. Maybe Caroline would say yes. Maybe she would. Maybe.

At the start of Third Avenue, I saw her. She was nearing the next intersection.

"Caroline!" I shouted.

She turned.

"Wait up!"

She did. She waited.

"Caroline," I said, all breathless when I got there. "I'm sorry. I want to be your friend again, and I'm sorry I was so horrible to you."

She looked at me and smiled. "Sure," she said.

"Sure what?"

"Sure I'll be friends with you again."

And I felt so good, I danced some of the steps I'd seen the other kids practice for "Poor Charlie." She danced them along with me. Up at the top of the hill, I saw Gabe. He was dancing the same exact steps. He disappeared when he saw me looking at him.

I stopped dancing. "How did you know that?" I asked Caroline. "How did you know those dance steps?"

"Mayella and Gabe taught me. They taught me the song, too. It's fun."

I looked back up the street and saw Gabe looking down again. He raised his arms skyward. I raised mine the same way. Then I noticed Caroline doing the same thing.

"Hey!" I dropped my arms. Caroline dropped hers, too, and Gabe ran off down a side street. "This is a setup," I said.

"Yep." Caroline grinned a wide grin. "So?" She started to laugh. "So?"

I laughed, too. It was perfect. TracyanCaroline, Carolinean-Tracy.

Laughing, we went down to my house and had some oat-meal cookies and hot chocolate. The kind so thick it's almost a pudding. The kind only Pa can make.

17.

Peter stood before our music class wearing only a muddy bathing suit.

"Woo-woo," called Avi. "Whoop-whoop-whoop!"

The rest of the class joined in with whistles and general rowdiness.

We bowed.

"Thank you very much," Peter called through the noise. "That concludes our skit. Please leave contributions at the door."

Everything had gone well. I'd played the incidental music while the other kids, including Caroline (no one told us we couldn't use extras, Mayella had pointed out), covered the speaking parts. Then we reached Peter's poem.

"Poor Charlie," the other four sang, "poor Charlie, the boy his mother made of mud!"

WAPWAPWAP! The mud just flew from the buckets to Peter's chest.

By the time we got to the end of the skit, there was mud all over the place, and the kids in their desks were screaming with laughter. And I was laughing, too. Laughing hard.

"She's laughing," said Peter.

"I know it," said Gabe. "Go ahead. Give it your best shot."

And WAP!

One more handful of mud hit Gabe full on the chest.

Later, after talking and giggling half the night, I lay in my sleeping bag on the living-room floor. I listened to the soft breathing of Mayella and Caroline. My friends.

Everything felt so wonderful. Mayella and Caroline and Pa and Gabe and Peter and Toni and the bird's nest and Monkey Rock. I wanted to keep this feeling. I knew if I stayed where I was, warm and snug, I would fall asleep, so I inched out of the sleeping bag and tiptoed to the front door. As I went past the couch, I grabbed the afghan and wrapped it around myself.

Quietly, quietly, I opened the door. I sat on one of the porch steps and watched the moonlit street. So quiet and silvery and cold, but the afghan kept me warm enough. For a few quiet minutes it would. Warm enough and a little afraid, but it was so beautiful there. And if I got too afraid, the door to the house was right behind me.

Then I forgot to feel afraid. I didn't have room for that in my heart. I was happy. Just happy.

"Tracy," whispered the breeze, and I knew it wasn't Mama. Not really. But I felt her, and I gathered in the moonlight and the honeysuckle rose and the warmth of her breath.

"Mama," I whispered back. "I miss you."

"I'm here," came the reply.

I closed my eyes while she held me safe in her arms, her lips on my cheek. I nestled against her breast while she said in the softest voice,

Always
I will be your mother,

Long into the spill of time
And when time no longer
Has anything to do with
Dawn or dark.

I will be your mother
Among the oranges,
The local newspapers
And the rattling of cat-bird songs

You can grow up
Wild and bright.
You can be wind
Or fire,
Willow
Or oak
You can breathe green.
You can wear poppies
In your hair.
You can stand astonished
In the moonlight
Or peek from a safe,
Moonless space—
I will be your mother

I may turn into sky
Or red clay
Or simply bones.
I may become delicate
As milkweed

Or hammered hard
As canyon cleft
But I will be
Your mother.

Yes.

Always.

And with Mama locked safely in my heart and the thing that was shattered mended, I tiptoed back inside.